SAVING LILIANA

BROTHERHOOD PROTECTORS YELLOWSTONE
BOOK FOUR

ELLE JAMES

TWISTED PAGE INC

SAVING LILIANA

BROTHERHOOD PROTECTORS
YELLOWSTONE BOOK #4

New York Times & *USA Today*
Bestselling Author

ELLE JAMES

Dedicated to my friend Bev for being the beautiful, smart, sexy, loving person she is. I am truly blessed to call her my friend.
Elle James

AUTHOR'S NOTE

Enjoy other military books by Elle James

Brotherhood Protectors Yellowstone

Visit ellejames.com for more titles and release dates
Join her newsletter at
https://ellejames.com/contact/

CHAPTER 1

"I'M NOT HERE to make empty promises. I'm here because I care what happens to our country, our great state of Wyoming and the people who live here. You are why I'm campaigning for U.S. Congress. I promise to represent you and what you want for our country, state and people of all races. I'm Liliana Lightfeather, born and raised here in Wyoming, one hundred percent American and one hundred percent Shoshone. I will represent *you*. Please, get out and vote for the one person who will have your best interests at heart." Liliana stood tall, her shoulders back, chin held high, projecting the confidence needed to win the election.

Back when she'd been a struggling high school student, if anyone had asked her whether she'd ever run for a political office, she would have said no way in hell. Yet here she was a dozen years later, doing just that. If the polls were right, she had a real chance at winning the election. She just had to keep up the momentum until election day, which meant traveling all over the state, connecting with her constituents, and thus, putting a face to the name on the ballot.

She smiled, answered questions and finally held up her hand. "Thank you for coming out to greet me. Please, vote. If not for me, then for the candidate of your choice. It's important for every voice to be heard."

She turned and started down the steps of the outdoor stage, waving with one hand and holding the handrail with the other.

When Liliana was only halfway down the steps, the stage behind her exploded. The force of the blast sent her flying down the remainder of the wooden steps, where she landed on the pavement and skidded on her hands and knees before coming to a full stop, face-down on the asphalt.

Women screamed, and people ran past her.

Liliana lay still, trying to make sense out of what had tossed her to the ground. When she lifted her head, blood trickled down her forehead into her eye. She pushed to a sitting position and brushed the blood away, touching her fingers to its source. Her hands and knees burned, and her new black suit jacket was torn at the elbow.

"Liliana!" Amanda Small ran toward her and dropped down to her knees. "Are you all right? Oh, sweetie, you're bleeding." Her friend and fellow tribeswoman fumbled in her handbag, pulled out her cell phone and punched in three numbers. "Yes, this is Amanda Small. I'm at the Riverton town square. There's been an explosion. Please, send an ambulance. ASAP!"

Liliana laid her scraped hand on her friend's arm. "I don't need an ambulance. I'm okay."

Amanda frowned, her phone still at her ear. "Good. The sooner they get here, the better." She ended the call and looked at Liliana. "First responders are on their way." She dug in her purse again, pulled out a small package of tissues, tore it open and pressed one to the wound on Liliana's forehead.

Liliana winced. "Ouch."

Amanda grimaced. "Sorry. Didn't mean to cause you more pain. Just trying to stop the bleeding." She gripped Liliana's hand and lifted it to the tissue over the wound. "Apply steady pressure. The bleeding should stop soon. And we need to get you somewhere safe."

Liliana pressed gently on the tissue as she glanced around at the thinning crowd. "Is anyone else hurt? We should get everyone away from the stage. We don't know if that was the only explosion."

A man was helping one of the members of the tribal council up from the ground. The councilman appeared dazed but able to stand on his own.

After a quick inventory and test of all her limbs, Liliana lurched to her feet.

"Normally, I'd say you shouldn't get up, but I don't want to stand around and wait for something else to explode," Amanda said. "I worry, that you hit your head. What if you've suffered an injury to your spinal cord?"

"I'm okay," Liliana said, stepping past Amanda and heading for the injured older man she recognized as Bill Running Bear.

"Bill, are you okay?" she asked.

He nodded and winced, touching a hand to his head. "What happened?"

A member of the tribal police force hurried forward. "Someone set off explosives beneath the stage." He nodded toward the platform Liliana had been standing on moments before. "Everyone needs to move away from the stage."

"Wow," Amanda said, her eyes wide as they moved away from the blast zone. "If you'd talked a few minutes longer, that could've been you." She lifted her chin toward the rubble that was left of the wooden stage that had been erected for Liliana's campaign speech.

The blood rushed from Liliana's head, and her knees wobbled.

"Thank you for being brief and to the point," Amanda whispered.

The tribal police officer nodded. "A long-winded

candidate wouldn't have survived that. Or, at the very least, would've been terribly hurt."

Liliana shook her head and regretted it immediately. She raised a hand to pinch the bridge of her nose. "Who would do such a thing?"

A siren sounded, increasing in volume as it neared the center of town where they'd set up amid the craft show that always accompanied the annual county fair at the edge of town.

Liliana's vision blurred, and she swayed.

Amanda brought her arm up around her waist. "Steady. You are definitely going to see a doctor. You were one of the closest to the explosion."

"I'm okay," Liliana insisted, though her voice didn't hold as much conviction as she'd have liked. "I'm just sick."

Amanda turned her head left and right. "Let's find you a place to sit."

"Not that kind of sick." Liliana sighed. "I'm sick that because someone decided to sabotage my stage, others have been injured."

"You didn't set off the explosion. Sweetie, this wasn't your fault," Amanda said.

"I know that, but the people injured were gathered to see me. I feel responsible, even if I didn't set those charges. Because I was here, I endangered the lives of those good people who came to hear me talk."

Amanda's lips pressed into a thin line. "This isn't

the first time someone has tried to sabotage your campaign."

Liliana sighed. "I know. I gave the curtain collapse in that theater in Casper the benefit of the doubt."

"Then the sprinkler system going off in the conference center in Laramie..." Amanda reminded her.

Her fist tightened. "That could've been faulty sensors or something." Liliana shook her head. "But this—"

"Was a downright deadly attack that could've gotten someone killed," Amanda finished, her frown deepening. She lifted her cell phone and scrolled through her contacts.

"Who are you calling now?" Liliana wanted to know.

"I'm calling in the big guns," she said, her voice steely, her expression resolute.

Liliana shook her head, the motion causing her to sway dizzily. "What big guns?"

"The Brotherhood Protectors."

Liliana's eyes narrowed. "The group of mercenaries Carter works with?"

Amanda's tight countenance softened.

A stab of envy hit Liliana square in the gut. Her friend, Amanda, had fallen for Carter Manning, a former Navy SEAL, working with a group of mercenaries out of West Yellowstone, Montana, the Brotherhood Protectors.

"They *were* mercenaries," Amanda corrected. "Now they're protectors, bodyguards, extraction specialists. Whatever it takes to help people in tight places."

"Like you?" Liliana smiled weakly at her friend.

Amanda's lips turned up on the corners. "Like me." She pointed a finger at Liliana. "And you. Based on what's occurred on your campaign trail, it appears you need protection."

Liliana shook her head. "I just can't believe someone would go to all this trouble to eliminate me as competition."

"Sweetie, believe it." Amanda tipped her head toward the destroyed stage. "Your campaign was five feet away from ending today." Her eyes narrowed as her focus shifted to her cell phone. "Carter, we could use some help here in Riverton." She turned away as she filled in her fiancé on what was going on.

Liliana strained to eavesdrop but was distracted by the arrival of the ambulance as it pulled into the town square. Emergency Medical Technicians leaped out, grabbed their gear and headed toward her.

As the EMTs approached, Liliana pointed to Bill. "He needs help."

Over the next hour, Liliana and Amanda moved around the square, helping identify those needing medical assistance. She, Amanda and others spoke with law enforcement about the explosion, giving what details they could.

Once all injured parties were evaluated, Amanda led an EMT to Liliana. "She needs you to look at her. Don't let her tell you differently. She's stubborn to a fault." Amanda's eyes narrowed at Liliana. "Don't give them any trouble, or you'll have to answer to me."

Liliana chuckled and gave Amanda a salute. "I think you missed your calling. You should've been a drill sergeant or a prison matron."

Amanda lifted her chin. "I'm a teen counselor. A much more difficult calling."

"Right." Liliana laughed. "You meet the criteria of all the above."

Amanda propped her fists on her hips. "Damn right."

The medical technician performed a quick evaluation, shining a light into Liliana's eyes and checking her vital signs. "I recommend you see a doctor. We can transport you in the ambulance if you like."

Liliana was shaking her head even before the man finished his sentence. "I feel fine."

"Head injuries can be tricky," the EMT said. "One minute, you might feel fine. The next, you might be comatose or dead due to a brain bleed. It's always good to have a doctor check you out."

Liliana smiled at the technician. "Your concern is noted. I'll do that."

Amanda stood next to her with her arms crossed over her chest. "When?"

"When I have time." Liliana nodded toward the EMT. "Thank you."

The man carried his medical bag back to the ambulance, climbed into the cab, closed the door and the truck pulled away.

Amanda checked her cell phone. "Come on. We have a plane to catch."

Liliana blinked. "A what?"

"A plane," Amanda said. "You know, one of those flying objects with wings?" She hooked Liliana's arm and led her toward her parked car.

"I'm due in Cody tomorrow for the next campaign speech. It's only a two-hour drive...max."

"While you were playing Florence Nightingale, I called Rachel and told her what was going on. I had her call the Mayor of Cody to tell him you'd have to reschedule your visit there for another time."

Liliana ground to a halt and tugged her arm free of Amanda's hold. "You did what?"

"I had Rachel postpone your Cody visit until we get a handle on your safety." Amanda's cell phone dinged, indicating an incoming text. She glanced down. "That's Rachel. The mayor understood and will make room on the city calendar when you're ready to come through."

Liliana glared at Amanda. "Don't I have a say in all of this?"

"Of course you do. As long as you agree with me." Amanda cocked her head to one side and lifted a single eyebrow. "Now, will you come with me willingly, or do I have to throw you over my shoulder and carry you to the car?"

Liliana laughed out loud. At five feet three inches, Amanda couldn't throw Liliana, who was four inches taller, over her shoulder. "I'd crush you."

Amanda's brow rose even higher. "Try me."

Liliana glanced around at the emptying square and sighed. "Okay. But where are we going? You said plane. Last I knew, you had to drive to Cheyenne or Denver for any decent commercial flights. And where would we be flying to?"

Amanda hooked Liliana's arm again and led her toward the parked cars. "Carter's boss arranged for a private plane to collect us at the Riverton Airport. They're flying us to West Yellowstone, where their organization's regional headquarters is located."

"It's only a two-hour drive," Liliana protested. "Why fly?"

Amanda stopped in front of her SUV, unlocked the door and held it for Liliana to get in. "We're worried about you being exposed on the road without anyone to protect you."

"Seriously?" Liliana bit her bottom lip. "You think someone would try to attack me while I'm driving?"

"After today's explosion?" Amanda nodded. "At this point, I wouldn't even get into your own car. Carter notified the Wyoming State Police bomb squad. They're on their way to check it out as we speak."

Liliana glanced toward her SUV parked a few spaces away.

A member of the tribal police was placing yellow caution tape around her black SUV.

"Until the bomb squad has checked out your vehicle, we must assume it's not safe." Amanda touched her arm. "If someone was desperate enough to plant explosives under your stage, they might've used the confusion to plant more under your car."

An icy chill rippled down Liliana's spine. "What have I done to make someone mad enough to want me dead?" Liliana whispered as she sank into the passenger seat of Amanda's SUV.

"I don't know, but I'm not trained to protect you. Fortunately, Carter's team is. We're going to meet with them." Amanda closed Liliana's door and rounded the front of her vehicle to the driver's side.

"We?" Liliana turned to Amanda as she slid behind the wheel. "What about your work? You can't be gone for days. Those kids need you."

"I'll only be gone for the rest of the day. I was off from work anyway to be here with you." She smiled as she started the engine and backed out of the parking space. "I'll fly back later this evening."

"Wow." Liliana shook her head, dizzy from everything happening around her, more so than from the bump on her head. "This is almost too much to take in. I'm running for a seat in the house, not for the presidency. Why target me?"

"Someone must think you have a chance of winning." Amanda's lips pressed together. "And they don't want that to happen...at all costs." She glanced in the mirror, hesitating to shift into drive.

Liliana glanced around. "What are you waiting for?"

"Jason Murphy promised to give us a police escort to the airport."

"Oh." Liliana sighed as a Riverton Police Department SUV pulled in behind them. "It all seems overly dramatic."

Amanda cast a glance toward Liliana. "Five feet."

She'd been five feet away from dying that day.

Liliana sat silently as Amanda drove to the airport. As they pulled up to the terminal, a small jet landed on the tarmac and taxied to the terminal.

"I think that's our ride." Amanda shifted into park and got out.

Liliana joined her in front of the SUV, looking around, half-expecting someone to jump out of the shadows to attack. When no one did, she shook her head. Still, she was glad when Jason Murphy left his SUV and escorted them into the building and out the other side to the waiting plane.

A man lowered the stairs, stepped out of the plane and onto the tarmac.

Amanda grinned. "Carter!" She ran to the man and flung her arms around him.

Liliana's heart warmed for the first time since the explosion. She and Amanda had been friends since high school. Liliana had never seen her friend happier. Even the tug of envy tightening her chest couldn't make her less ecstatic that Amanda had found the love of her life.

Liliana had been busy fighting the odds of her birthright to get to where she was so far. So many of her people never left the reservation. Those who stayed faced lives of unemployment, alcoholism and drug abuse. When her father had died in a fatal car crash, driving drunk, Liliana's mother had scraped out a living by cleaning rooms at the casino during the day and working in a bar at night to provide for Liliana.

Liliana remembered how tired her mother had been and vowed to make something of herself so that she could take care of the mother who'd done so much for her.

And she *had* made something of herself. She'd gone to college on scholarships and worked part-time jobs to pay for her room and board, refusing to take money from her mother. She'd graduated at the top of her class, applied to law school and had been accepted. She'd worked her way through law school then interned with a firm in Denver and with a congressman from Wyoming in Washington, D.C.

Later, she'd worked for a law firm in Cheyenne, gaining experience and helping the people of her tribe and others navigate the justice system's complexities. These last few years, she'd fought to protect reservation land holdings and Yellowstone National Park from being pushed around by big corporations hungry to get their hands on rights of way and the natural resources within.

Carter Manning kissed Amanda soundly before stepping back to face Liliana. He held out his hand. "You must be the candidate."

Amanda slipped an arm around his waist and waved a hand toward Liliana. "Carter Manning, this is Liliana Lightfeather, Wyoming's best candidate for the U.S. House of Representatives." She grinned.

"I don't know about best, but I like to think I have the best interests of the state at heart." Liliana gripped Carter's hand in a firm handshake. "Nice to finally meet the man who saved my friend from the drug cartel and put a smile on her face."

He nodded. "Amanda has nothing but good things to say about you, Miss Lightfeather."

"Please, call me Liliana." She looked past him to the plane. "Are you flying this?"

He laughed. "Not hardly. My skills aren't in flying the plane. I could jump out of it with a parachute and land without breaking all the bones in my body, but flying?" He shook his head. "I'll leave that to the pilot. He's waiting to take us to West Yellowstone."

Liliana tipped her head. "Why West Yellowstone?"

"Stone Jacobs would have come to meet you here himself," Carter said, "but we thought it might be a good idea to remove you from the area altogether until we get a security plan in place." He grinned. "And I asked to fly out. Gives me a little more time with Amanda."

Amanda leaned into him. "I'm glad you came. This long-distance relationship is getting old. Are you done with your assignment? Please tell me you were successful."

He nodded. "Got the little girl back from her father, who'd absconded with her to Canada. She's back with her mother, and Canada is sending him back to face kidnapping charges."

Amanda sighed. "I'm glad she's home. I can't imagine what her mother went through." She hooked Liliana's arm and turned her toward the plane. "See? The people Carter works with do good things, saving little kids and protecting people like me from drug cartels, stalkers and murderers. I'm positive they can help see you through the rest of your campaign."

"That's the idea," Carter confirmed behind her. "Stone already has our computer genius scouring the internet for information that could help identify people who might have something against you. He's researching your opposition and pouring through court records of cases you represented. They'll have questions for you when you get to the lodge."

"What if I don't want to go with your organization? I might not be able to afford your services," Liliana said. "You could be wasting your time."

Carter grinned. "That's the beauty of the Brotherhood Protectors. The man who started it, Hank Patterson, will help whether you can afford it or not. He and his wife, Sadie McClain, set up a foundation to help those who can't afford to hire a bodyguard."

Amanda nodded. "I sure as hell couldn't afford a bodyguard on what they pay me on the reservation. I didn't have to worry. They assigned Carter, no questions asked, no money required." She led the way up the stairs into the plane. "I wouldn't be here today otherwise."

Liliana climbed the steps and entered the plane, her breath catching at the luxurious interior. "Does this plane belong to the Brotherhood Protectors?"

Carter laughed. "No. Hank has connections. When he asks for help, they come through."

"It also helps that his wife is a huge star," Amanda said.

Liliana frowned. "*The* Sadie McClain? You're serious?"

Carter nodded. "He knew her back when she was just a girl from Montana. She was his first love and his first case post-military and the reason he started the Brotherhood Protectors. She had a stalker trying to kill her." He shook his head. "It turned out the stalker was her sister-in-law."

"I read something about that." Liliana sank into a buttery-soft, white leather seat.

"Now, they're happily married with two children, and the Brotherhood Protectors has expanded to include three locations." Carter pulled the stairs up and locked the door. He passed Liliana on his way to the cockpit, where he gave the pilot a thumbs up.

The engine fired up, and soon, they were taxiing to the end of the runway.

Liliana's fingers dug into the leather armrests as the plane lifted off the ground.

What had started as just another day on the campaign trail had ended in an explosion and a ride in a plush jet to meet with people who would provide protection she never thought she'd need.

Someone had an issue with her and the platform on which she'd based her campaign. Yes, the explosion had scared her, making her aware of her vulnerability, but it hadn't beaten her.

If there was one thing she'd learned growing up on the rez...when you got knocked down, you got up and got the hell back in the fight.

She'd be damned if someone thought they could scare her into dropping out of the race. Her tribe and the people of Wyoming needed her to represent their best interests. She was more determined than ever to win.

If it meant taking on a bodyguard to see her through to election day, so be it.

CHAPTER 2

DAXTON YOUNG HAD BEEN out on horseback for two hours when he got the text message from his boss, Stone Jacobs.

Need you back at the lodge ASAP. Got a new client.

Since arriving in West Yellowstone, he'd assisted on a couple of assignments but had yet to go solo. He noted that the text had been sent almost an hour earlier. With reception spotty at best this far away from town, he hadn't gotten it immediately. He reined around the dappled gray appaloosa named Pepper and started back, taking a more direct route than the one he'd followed, meandering along the Madison River.

He'd taken up riding since he'd come to Grand Yellowstone Lodge with his team. Having grown up on military bases, he'd done some riding at the base stables but none since he'd joined the Navy as soon as he'd graduated high school.

The sooner he'd been able to get out of his father's house, the better for himself and his father. The man had had no patience for a teenage boy—and a rebellious one at that. Hell, he'd had no patience for Dax at any age since he'd taken over as his only parent when Dax had been five years old.

He'd known his father as his father's troops had known him. Master Gunny, an integral cog in the machine pushing out kids like Dax from recruits to Marines.

Master Gunny hadn't cut Dax any more slack than he had the other recruits. He hadn't shown any more affection either. Sometimes, Dax had felt his father blamed him for being stuck in the training command because he hadn't been able to deploy, being a single parent with a small child and no backup to watch Dax should he be gone for months on end.

The animosity he'd felt from his father had started the day his mother had 'died.' It hadn't been until he was fifteen that he'd learned his mother hadn't died but had abandoned them, leaving Master Gunny to raise his son alone.

Since learning of his mother's betrayal, Dax couldn't trust women. Yes, he'd dated, but not for long. And he'd never married. Most of the guys he knew were divorced after their first deployment. Why bother? Women couldn't be trusted.

As Dax cleared a stand of trees, he nudged Pepper into a gallop, eating up the distance between them and the lodge. Before long, the town of West Yellowstone came into view.

The Grand Yellowstone Lodge stood on the edge of town. Dax didn't have to ride through the streets to get to the lodge or the barn behind it.

As he neared the barn, he slowed Pepper to a trot and then to a walk, allowing the animal to cool down before coming to a complete halt. Yes, he needed to get back ASAP, but not at the expense of the animal. He respected the creature and would do right by it. Stone would wait. Of all people, he'd understand.

His boss was more of a teammate than a manager. Even when they'd worked as highly trained mercenaries in Afghanistan, Stone had insisted they were a team. Dax would follow the man anywhere. He wasn't just a teammate. Like the other members, they were brothers.

Now, they were brothers working with the Brotherhood Protectors, not in Afghanistan as hired bodyguards for corporate representatives working on reconstruction contracts.

Already, the team had worked protecting a wolf biologist and a teen counselor on the Wind River Reservation. Most recently, they'd been on a recovery mission to Canada to retrieve a child kidnapped by her father. At first, Dax hadn't been sure he'd want to stay in the remote location of West Yellowstone or how much work could be found for the team.

What they'd done so far made him believe in their worth and eager to help in any situation. With gaps between assignments, he'd filled his time relearning how to ride and care for horses. He helped in the barn and the lodge where help was needed, which was a good thing since he'd never been one to kick back and relax.

During his rebellious teens, his father had made it a point to say Dax was too much like his mother, too flighty and never able to sit still. As an adult looking back, he realized he'd picked up more of his father's traits than he'd realized. He had to keep moving but be productive in the process.

Riding horses was as sedentary as he got. And he'd found a sense of peace in the process. So, it wasn't being still, but he got away from the noise of the town and found a sense of calm he had never known. Horseback riding at the military base stables had come close, but he'd still been surrounded by the sights and sounds of other people, machinery, aircraft and highways.

When he rode away from West Yellowstone, he could get far enough away from town and the highways that he only heard the sound of the horse's hooves hitting the hard-packed earth.

His muscles tensed as he neared the barn and his

return to purpose and engagement.

John Jacobs met him at the door to the barn. "I'll take Pepper. Your team has gathered in the conference room in the loft. They're expecting you."

Dax frowned. "I take care of my own horse."

"Duly noted, but I'm sure Pepper won't mind this once." Stone's father winked. "Go on. I'll be sure to brush him and give him extra feed."

Dax dismounted and handed over the reins.

The barn had been empty when they'd first arrived at the lodge. No horses, no tack, no hay or sacks of feed.

The plan had been to convert the entire barn into another office for the Brotherhood Protectors.

They'd started the renovations in the loft, closing it off and insulating it for noise and weather. They'd all helped wiring it for electricity and computers, as well as adding a climate-controlled armory to store weapons, ammo and communications equipment.

What had been a drafty barn was now a state-of-the-art facility for the team operations. At least in the loft area.

Once back in his hometown, Stone had wanted to introduce his fiancée, Kyla, to the joys of country living, which meant riding horses and fishing. Which meant leaving the lower half of the barn as a barn.

She'd bought into the horseback riding but was still a work-in-progress when it came to fishing.

Stone had encouraged the others to take up riding

horses. In Montana and Wyoming, there were places they couldn't get to in a truck or SUV. They might be required to go in on horseback or ATVs.

Four-wheeler engines were nosier than horses and would give them away sooner. If they needed to sneak into a compound unannounced, they'd have to drop in via parachute or ride in on horseback.

Dax hadn't needed to be told twice. On horseback, he could get away and find the peace he'd only dreamed about.

He took the steps up to the loft two at a time, leaned close to the retinal scanner and waited for the application to recognize him and unlock the door.

When he heard the soft click, he pushed through the door and entered the freshly painted conference room.

The other five members of his original team were gathered around the large conference table. Three women had joined them. Kyla, the former CIA assassin and now an integral member of the Brotherhood Protectors, was there. She worked closely with Hank Paterson's computer guy, Swede, helping him with any data mining and research necessary for each operation. Kyla sat at the conference table, a keyboard in front of her, her monitor the large screen on the wall everyone could view from their seats at the table.

Amanda Small, Carter's woman, sat beside Carter, and next to her was a woman in a black blazer with hair much like Amanda's, black and as shiny as onyx. Unlike Amanda with her bright blue eyes, this woman had eyes so dark brown they rivaled the color of her hair and flashed as she turned her gaze on Dax.

"Dax," Stone said. "Good. The whole team's here. Carter, you want to give him the sitrep and bring him up to speed?"

Carter waved a hand toward the stranger with the black hair. "Our client is Liliana Lightfeather, an independent candidate running for congress in Wyoming. Today, the stage she'd been standing on exploded. The explosion, plus two other disturbing incidents, lead us to believe someone doesn't like her or wants to scare her into bowing out of the race or kill her to keep her from winning."

Dax shot a glance toward the woman and noted the bruise on her forehead and the smudges of dirt ground into her black suit. "What did they use for explosives?"

"Just got word from the Wyoming State Police Bomb Squad that whoever set the charges used C-4."

Dax's eyebrows shot up. "C-4 is a controlled substance, not available to just anyone."

Kyla nodded. "Swede and I are searching the internet for any news regarding recent thefts of C-4 as well as hoping to identify buyers who might have quantities on hand, so we can have them conduct inventories to ensure they haven't experienced pilfering. It will take time to locate a possible source of the C-4."

"In the meantime, I can't stop campaigning," Liliana Lightfeather sat up straight, her head held high. "If the person or persons behind the attacks is trying to scare me into withdrawing from the race, it won't happen. The voters have the right to determine who will represent them at the national level."

"What about the incumbent?" Dax asked.

"She was recently diagnosed with a brain tumor and announced her retirement so she can focus on beating cancer and spending time with her family," Liliana said. "Wyoming only has one seat in the House of Representatives as it's the smallest state, not in land size, but in population."

Dax's eyes narrowed. "And the other candidates?"

"Ronald Merritt, the GOP's pick to replace the current congresswoman," Kyla offered.

"And Brad Benton, the Democratic candidate," Liliana added.

"If you weren't running as an independent, who is most likely to win?" Stone asked.

"Ronald Merritt. The state leans toward conservative values," Liliana said.

"Then why would either party worry about an independent running?"

Amanda sat forward. "Merritt leans too far to the right with his stance on abortion and limiting women's rights, and Benton leans too far to the left, wanting to shut down mining and the pipelines, taking away what few job opportunities are available in the state." She grinned. "Liliana is leading in the latest polls, with enough of a lead to make both parties worry."

"If she wasn't leading in the polls by a significant margin, the republicans would be worrying she'd take votes away from them and give the democratic candidate a shot at the seat." Stone tapped his fingers on the tabletop. "As it stands, she's leading by a lot more than they had anticipated and could steal the election from their candidate altogether."

"Wouldn't that make the GOP candidate and his party the prime suspects in the attacks?" Dax asked.

"Seems logical," Stone agreed. "Or that candidate's corporate backers—the ones contributing the most money to Merritt's campaign." Stone tipped his head toward the empty chair across from Liliana Lightfeather. "Have a seat."

Dax glanced down at his dusty jeans and scratched his beard. "I'm dirty from riding."

"Is that what I smell?" Moe laughed.

"Sit," Stone insisted. "The seats can be cleaned. We want your input on how to handle Miss Lightfeather's situation."

"I would've thought you'd come up with something by now." Dax dropped into the seat, a frown forming. "Shouldn't she lay low until you figure out who's behind the attacks?"

Miss Lightfeather shook her head, her jaw firm, her fists clenched. "Laying low is the last thing I need to do at this point. I can't let them think they've won. I can't back down and make the voters think I can't stand the heat. If anything, the explosion will have given me even more exposure in the news. I have to show my opposition and voters that I'm uninjured, ready to take the fight to the next level and that I'm stronger than ever."

Amanda clapped her hands. "That's the spirit that will get you elected." She glanced around the table. "So, how can the Brotherhood Protectors make sure she stays alive through the election and into office?"

Stone turned to Liliana. "She needs protection."

Liliana's mouth twisted. "A bodyguard? Won't that make me appear weaker like I can't handle this election standing on my own two feet?"

"So many of our elected officials have bodyguards," Stone pointed out, "that I don't think it makes you appear weaker."

Her frown deepened. "I'm not opposed to having a bodyguard, but do we have to be so obvious about it? Couldn't I have someone follow me around like he's my aide or something?"

"We could. But you need closer protection than someone following you around during the day, like an aide. What you need is twenty-four-seven coverage. Someone who goes home with you at night and stays in at least adjoining rooms in whatever hotel you're staying in. If our guy isn't physically close, he can't protect you."

"I'm a single woman, which requires that I be very aware of my reputation. If I keep the bodyguard thing under wraps but have a man following me into my hotel room, the press will accuse me of sexual harassment, having an affair with my aide." Liliana shook her head. "I can't do that, and I don't want to parade around with a bodyguard like some celebrity. I'm a candidate of the people. I can't get close to them if they think I'm above them with my bodyguard."

Amanda laid her hand on Liliana's arm. "But you can get close to them with your fiancé."

Dax's gut tightened. He should have known a woman as attractive as Liliana would have a fiancé. Not that it should matter to him. The knot in his gut meant nothing. Certainly not disappointment.

"I don't have a fiancé." Liliana frowned.

Amanda smiled. "You know that and the rest of the people in this room know that, but the press and the voters don't know that. The explosion shook your secret boyfriend and made him realize just how much you mean to him. He spirited you away from Riverton and proposed to you. You accepted, and now, you'll have him with you for the rest of your campaign." Amanda grinned. "And your voters will be happy that you have the appearance of a stable homelife."

Liliana's brow dipped. "I can't lie to the people of

Wyoming. That's no way to serve them. And what happens when the election ends and my fiancé disappears?"

"You can make a public statement that your fiancé wasn't prepared for life in the public eye, and you parted amicably." Amanda sighed. "Or you just admit you needed a bodyguard. No one will hold it against you."

Liliana stared at her friend for a long time without uttering a word, as if working through the two scenarios.

"If you choose to have our protector as your bodyguard, wouldn't you have the same issue you'd have if he was your aide?" Kyla pointed out. "Wouldn't the press make something of your body-guard staying in adjoining rooms and sleeping in your house? You're a target of the press as much as you are a target of whoever is behind the attacks."

"Kyla's right," Stone said. "You can't think of it as lying to the public. You're guarding your reputation and life by having your protector go undercover. When the campaign is over, you can own up to that fact. Your voters will understand."

"And if your protector is your fiancé and not a highly-trained former special operations fighter, whoever is targeting you might get sloppy and expose himself for the sneaky bastard he is, and you'll have your fiancé to take him down." Amanda clapped her hand on the table. "So, who's Liliana's lucky guy?"

Stone glanced around at the men seated at the table as if sizing up each man as a potential fiancé for the congressional candidate.

His chest tight and blood pumping through his veins, Dax waited for Stone to decide. Stone, himself, had a fiancée in Kyla. If someone from West Yellowstone saw them on the news, they might out him. Same went for Bubba and Carter. They had fiancées, which left Dax, Moe and Hunter.

Dax glanced across the table at Liliana Lightfeather with her sleek dark hair and deep brown eyes.

Moe and Hunter might fall in love with the pretty congressional candidate and have a problem when they'd have to break up.

Having spent his life avoiding matrimony, Dax was the woman's best bet. He could walk away like he had so many times before. His deep distrust of the feminine gender would make the separation painless. And he'd find it challenging to go undercover and play the part.

He frowned at Stone. What was taking him so long to make up his mind? The longer the man deliberated, the tenser Dax grew. Finally, he laid his palm on the table. "I'll do it," he said at the same time as Moe said, "Send me."

Stone frowned. "We have two volunteers." He turned to Dax, drew a deep breath, and let it out. "You sure you can pull it off?"

Dax lifted his chin. "Why wouldn't I?"

Moe laughed. "You'll have to shower, for one. Can't go on the campaign trail smelling like a horse."

"Might want to shave the beard," Stone suggested.

Dax's Marine father had made him iron his shirts and jeans and maintain a clean shave and haircut. Dax knew how to look good in a uniform and civilian clothes. "I clean up well," he said. "I'll trim the beard."

"I clean up well too, and I don't have a beard," Moe insisted. "And I would have no problem pretending to be Miss Lightfeather's fiancé." He winked at her. "That would be the easy part."

Stone met Dax's gaze. "I admit, I had Moe in mind for this assignment, but given the potential to go undercover as Miss Lightfeather's fiancé, I think it should be the congressional candidate's choice who gets to be her fiancé." He turned to Liliana. "Who would you like to represent you as your fiancé? Will it be Daxton Young," he tipped his head toward Dax, "or Morris Cleveland?" Stone turned toward Moe.

Moe sat straighter in his seat, trying to appear taller than his five-foot-ten-inch height. "What I lack vertically, I make up for in huge personality." He grinned.

Liliana's gaze darted from Moe to Dax and back to Moe.

Dax's fingers curled into fists, and his breath

caught in his chest. For some incomprehensible reason, he wanted her to choose him.

He tried to tell himself it was because he was tired of waiting for work, but it was more than that. It was the deep, dark brown of her gaze that had captured him when he'd walked through the door and her desire, beyond her own safety, to be truthful to her constituents and do her best to represent all the people of her state.

For a long moment, her gaze rested on Moe, and her mouth softened into a smile. "Thank you both for volunteering to protect me. And Morris, as much as I appreciate your...personality...I'll go with Mr. Young." Liliana turned to Dax, her smile fading. "When can you start?"

Dax let go of the breath he'd been holding. "Immediately."

Her lips quirked, and her nose wrinkled. "And by immediately, I assume you mean after you shower."

The men around the table burst out laughing.

Stone clapped a hand to his back. "Dax, I believe you'll have your work cut out for you. We'll give you thirty minutes to shower and shave. Then you're on assignment until Miss Lightfeather is sworn into her position as Wyoming's newest congresswoman."

Dax pushed to his feet and nodded toward his new client, a rush of adrenaline coursing through his veins. "I'll only be fifteen minutes, tops."

"No hurry," Stone said. "There are enough of us

here to keep her safe while you get cleaned up. And if you need reinforcements at any time during your assignment, we've got your back. All you have to do is call."

"That's right," Carter said. "It took this team *and* Hank's to face the drug cartel when Amanda needed us most. We'll be there for you, too."

"Hopefully, it won't come to that." Dax looked around the table at the men he considered his brothers. "But it's good to know you have my six." His gaze went to his fake fiancée. "Miss Lightfeather," he said with a nod.

"Liliana," she corrected. "We can't be formal if we're supposed to be engaged."

"Liliana." He let her name flow across his lips, liking the way it felt and sounded. "You can call me Dax. No one calls me Daxton."

She nodded. "Dax." Her lips twisted again. "We don't have much time to get used to this charade. I've never been engaged, but surely it won't be too hard to pretend." Her brow wrinkled.

"That would make two of us." His lips quirked. "We'll learn together. Now, if you'll excuse me, I'll go wash the horse off me. I won't be long." He hurried away, wondering what the hell he'd just volunteered for.

What did he know about being engaged?

Absolutely nothing.

CHAPTER 3

"I TOLD you they'd come through for you." Amanda hooked her arm through Liliana's as they moved the meeting from the barn to the lodge dining room.

Liliana wasn't feeling quite as confident as Amanda. "Do I really have to pretend I have a fiancé? Is it necessary?"

"I think it's the most logical choice for your safety and reputation," Amanda insisted. "You know the press and your opponents have been watching, looking for dirt on you. All they need to see is a man, not your husband or fiancé, going into your hotel room, and they'll make you out as loose or accuse you of sexual harassment for taking advantage of a male employee."

"The key to undercover work is to make it convincing." Kyla fell in step beside her.

"And she knows," Stone said from behind the three women. "Kyla was undercover with the CIA."

Liliana stared at the woman with open admiration. "Was it hard to pretend to be someone you're not?"

"It's acting and embracing your role. Are you one hundred percent *you* when you get up in front of a crowd of people?" Kyla asked.

Liliana frowned. "I like to think I am. Then again...I'm not as confident as I project. At times, I feel like a fraud, and self-doubt creeps in."

"Do you let the crowd see that?" Kyla asked.

"Oh, hell no," Liliana said. "My campaign would've ended before it began."

"So, you put on an act," Kyla said. "It's better for you and them. They need you to represent them with confidence and conviction. So, you give them what they expect. You really want to help them, which is commendable, but you can't if you're not elected."

Liliana nodded slowly. "True."

"So, you do what you have to do to protect yourself, your reputation and make it through to election day." Kyla shrugged. "If you're convinced that you're doing the right thing, then fake it until you feel it." Kyla entered the dining room, found a seat close to Stone and rested her hand on her belly.

Liliana paused at the entrance to the dining room, leaned into Amanda and whispered. "I've been so busy with my career that I haven't had a significant relationship since high school and not much of one then. How do I fake something I've never felt?"

"You watch movies, don't you?" Amanda asked.

"Sometimes," Liliana said, "when I'm not reading law journals."

"Oh, sweetie," Amanda clucked her tongue. "You really do need to get out more often." She sighed. "How about this…treat it like standing up in front of a jury. You want them to buy into everything you have to say, so you appeal to their emotions, right?"

Liliana stood taller. "I state the facts."

Amanda nodded. "But you state them in a way that captures emotions. You want to sway the jury to agree with your arguments, right?"

"Absolutely." Liliana lifted her chin. "They have to really understand the importance of what I'm saying,"

"Using the same methods of demonstrating love as you see on television, build your case and present it like the defendant's life depends on it." Amanda's lips twisted. "The defendant being you, in this scenario." Amanda shook her head. "I can't believe I'm having to put this in lawyer speak to help you understand how to make people believe you're in love with Dax."

Liliana chuckled. "You're doing a pretty good job of it."

Amanda shrugged. "Bottom line, like Kyla said… fake it until you feel it. Acting is like a muscle. The more you do it, the easier it gets. Slip into the character...you in love with Dax."

Liliana's heart fluttered like it did her first day in court on a big, critical case. Only different. With the flutter of nerves came a surge of warmth she couldn't identify. The thought of pretending to be in love with Dax sent ripples of excitement through her.

She'd chosen Dax over Morris because she hadn't felt anything beyond indifference for the other man. When she'd glanced across the conference table at the man who'd come into the room smelling of the outdoors and horse, something had awakened inside her. It both frightened and exhilarated her at the same time. When she should have chosen Moe, who didn't inspire the same feeling, she found herself naming Dax.

She hoped her choice wasn't a big mistake. Should she win the election, she'd have her hands full with her campaign and her duties in office. Liliana didn't have the time nor the inclination to fall in love.

And since Dax was the hired help, the bodyguard on assignment to her, he wouldn't be in the market for some lovelorn woman, much less one who had chosen politics as her career. What man in his right mind would voluntarily get involved with a woman who would remain under a public microscope for years?

She followed Amanda into the dining room and claimed a seat at the large table near the swinging doors to the kitchen. Having been occupied with her speech that morning and standing in front of a crowd that day, food hadn't even crossed her mind.

Savory scents drifted through the kitchen doors into the dining room, making Liliana's stomach growl.

"Get ready for a culinary delight." Stone smiled. "The Grand Yellowstone lodge has one of the best cooks in the tri-state area of Montana, Wyoming and Idaho. How my father talked him into burying himself out here beats me."

"He's had free rein in the kitchen since he came to work with his father," Bubba said. "Not every restaurant is willing to allow their chef carte blanch. Cookie thrives on discovery and inventing new recipes." Bubba patted his midsection. "And we thrive on Cookie's meals." He headed for the swinging doors. "I'll see if he needs help."

As Bubba neared the door, it swung open in front of him. The big guy stepped back and grinned. "Perfect timing."

Three men emerged.

The first, John Jacobs, who had greeted her when she'd first arrived at the Grand Yellowstone Lodge, carried a large platter containing a scrumptious array of pork chops, grilled chicken breasts and steaks. "Hope you're hungry. Cookie's outdone himself yet again, and he might've cooked enough food for the entire county."

"Don't listen to him," said a shorter man with blue eyes and a shock of white hair, who followed John Jacobs carrying a heavy pot with a ladle. "If slabs of meat aren't your thing, this pot is full of my famous minestrone soup, full of vegetables and my secret flavoring."

"Mmm," Amanda licked her lips. "I've had Cookie's minestrone. It's better than he says."

"Tinker, did you get the tea?" Cookie asked without looking around.

"Only got two hands," came a voice from the kitchen. A wiry man with brown hair and brown eyes appeared, carrying a basket of bread rolls in one hand and a casserole dish filled with scalloped potatoes.

"Need me to bring out anything else?" Bubba asked.

"That pitcher of tea sitting on the counter," Cookie replied. "If you want anything stronger, you'll have to fend for yourself."

Bubba disappeared into the kitchen and returned seconds later, carrying the large pitcher of tea. He made a trip around the table, filling glasses full of the clear brown liquid before taking his own seat.

Talk turned to prior assignments and what was happening in their personal lives. Liliana enjoyed listening to their stories and good-natured ribbing.

John Jacob gave his son a curt chin lift. "You two set a date yet?"

Stone shot a glance toward Kyla. "I'd get it done this week if I could get my fiancée to go along with a courthouse wedding."

"No way," Kyla said. "I want the white dress, flowers and first dance. I'll let you know the date as soon as I find the dress and a place to host the event."

"That baby will get here before you find a venue," Amanda said. "I've heard you have to plan a year out to get on venue schedules."

"Seriously?" Kyla shook her head and rubbed her small, slightly rounded belly,

"You're pregnant," Liliana exclaimed.

"*We* are," Stone confirmed.

Kyla laughed. "Though I'm carrying the baby, it took two to get this far. So, yes, we're pregnant."

"And still waiting for a wedding date," Stone repeated with a cocked eyebrow.

"Don't push it, buster," Kyla warned with a narrow-eyed glare. "I accepted your proposal at a weak moment. Don't make me regret it."

Stone chuckled as he raised his hands. "Backing off. When you're ready, you'll let me know."

Kyla sighed. "I will. This girl is only getting married once. I want to do it right."

"Let me know what I can do to help," Amanda offered."

"Know a venue where we can tie the knot?" Kyla grimaced. "He's due in six months. Seems like time is flying by. I haven't even started getting ready for him." She shoved a hand through her hair and looked around as if trying to find a carbon copy of herself to accomplish everything she needed to do.

"We have a community hall on the rez, but you have to be at least a quarter Shoshone or Arapaho to use it. Have you considered flying to Vegas and getting married in one of the chapels there?"

Kyla cocked an eyebrow. "How about it, big guy? We could have Elvis officiate."

Stone's brow dipped. "Hell no."

Kyla pouted, the look so foreign on the former CIA agent Liliana had to smother a giggle. "Spoilsport," Kyla muttered. "I always swore I couldn't be with a guy who didn't appreciate Elvis."

"I'm a huge Elvis fan," Stone argued. "Sadly, the king is dead, not out for a donut. The impersonators are a little creepy to me."

Kyla shrugged. "Going to Vegas would get it done, as you so nicely put it. And our son wouldn't be born a bastard."

"We will be married before our *daughter* is born, come hell or high water."

Kyla tilted her head. "Hell or high water...what does that even mean? I've heard that saying all my life, and it makes little sense to me."

Moe nodded, his face straight, serious. "One of the great mysteries of life."

Footsteps sounded across the wooden floor, and all gazes turned toward the man entering the room.

Liliana swiveled in her seat.

Dax strode into the dining room, his dark damp hair slicked back from his forehead. He wore a crisp white button-down, long-sleeved shirt, black trousers and brown dingo boots. He'd trimmed his beard neatly and scrubbed away all traces of dirt he'd accumulated during his earlier ride. To top it all off, he carried a black leather jacket over his shoulder. The result was an extremely, albeit ruggedly, handsome man who stole Liliana's breath away.

She tore her glance away from Dax and looked toward Moe, the man she'd passed on.

Nope.

He didn't steal her breath away and would likely have been the safer choice of the two men.

Her gaze slipped back to Dax, and those same warning bells clanged loudly in her head.

How would she function on the campaign trail with this bearded hunk at her side pretending to be her one true love? He didn't even have to open his mouth, and Liliana was already halfway in love with him.

She closed her eyes and gave herself a stern, internal scolding.

Lust.

What you're feeling is lust. Don't mistake lust for love. You are a professional, soon to be a legislator, who has to walk a very narrow line of morality to keep your constituents from bailing on you.

Liliana squared her shoulders, opened her eyes and met his gaze. "Better."

His lips quirked on the corner. "Glad you approve." He glanced around the table.

Amanda jumped up from her seat. "You should sit here and get to know your fiancée better. Might as well start now."

"Don't—" Liliana grabbed Amanda's arm, panic threatening to overwhelm her. She wasn't ready for this. She wasn't cut out for acting like she was in love with a man she barely knew.

Amanda smiled down at her and unhooked Liliana's grip on her arm. "You're in good hands. Dax will take care of you. However, if you want the charade to work, you have to get to know enough about each other to appear legit. The press will want to know all the details, including how he proposed." Amanda grinned. "Make him do it right."

"But he didn't and isn't," Liliana protested.

Amanda patted her hand. "Of course, he didn't and won't propose. The press doesn't have to know that. Give them what they want...a great story and make sure yours matches Dax's. You don't want to be called out on a lie." She winked and rounded the chairs to the other side of the dining table, where she slipped into the seat beside Carter.

Liliana was glad Amanda was spending her time with Carter. Until he moved to Riverton, they'd have to split their time between West Yellowstone and the

Wind River Indian Reservation. Amanda wouldn't leave the rez when so many young people were unemployed and feeling hopeless. They needed her more than Carter needed her. That he understood her desire to give back to her people was more than most men would concede.

Yeah, Amanda was lucky she'd found Carter, and he was lucky to have Amanda's love. She practically glowed with the emotion.

Liliana's face heated as Dax dropped into the seat beside her and filled his plate with food from the platters.

Once he had something from every platter, he dug his fork in and ate every last bite, never uttering a word.

Liliana studied him out of the corner of her eye while the others at the table laughed and joked about past events, personalities and future assignments.

Dax laid down his fork and picked up the can of beer he'd been nursing through his meal. He downed the brew, drew a deep breath and glanced around the table, his gaze coming to rest on Liliana. "Are you ready to get started? We have a lot to cover in a short amount of time."

Her heart skipped several beats. "What do you propose?" As soon as she uttered the word, she wished she hadn't. Heat flamed in her cheeks, and she looked away.

"About that…" Dax dropped to one knee and held out his hand.

"Oh, he's going to do it for real," Amanda cried. "Smart. It will be easier to remember the action than just an empty script. Go, Dax!"

Dax smiled. "As Amanda so loudly proclaimed, action is much easier to remember than words. In front of our family and friends, I want to proclaim my devotion and ask this one question… Will you marry me? And by marry me, I mean, do you promise to pretend to be my fiancée for as long as we both shall live or need to pretend we're engaged…whichever comes first?"

The heat in her face burned as she stared down at Dax's serious face. The urge to run had never been greater. Yet she remained glued to the spot, imagining Dax's proposal was the real thing.

Amanda cleared her throat. "Are you going to respond?"

"Yes, of course." Liliana shook free of the fantasies flitting through her mind. Fantasies of love, marriage and children with thick brown hair and gorgeous blue eyes like their father's. Pure fantasy. It wasn't like that would ever happen. He wasn't interested, and she didn't have time.

Squaring her shoulders, she lifted her chin. "Yes, I promise to do the best I can to convince others we are a couple destined for the altar until the danger has passed."

"You'll have to come up with a ring," Kyla said. "People always want to see the ring."

"I think I can help you with that." John Jacobs stood. "I have a ring in the safe we found when we were remodeling one of the guest bedrooms. It was covered in dust and pretty dirty, but it cleaned up beautifully. I had a jeweler verify it's a real diamond."

Liliana frowned. "I can't take your ring."

John waved her protest aside and hurried out of the room. He was back in less than three minutes with the ring, a simple band with a marquis diamond. "It's not fancy, but it should do the trick."

Dax took the ring from John.

Liliana pushed to her feet and raised her hands in protest. "I can't. I'd feel awful if I lost or damaged it."

"Don't worry about it," John said. "It didn't cost me anything. And if it helps keep you safe, I'll consider it having gone to a good cause."

Liliana hesitated a moment longer. "Well, if you're sure you don't want to sell it, I'll take care of it and return it to you as soon as the danger is passed."

She held out her hand for the ring.

Instead of handing her the ring, Dax turned over her hand and slid the ring onto her left ring finger.

A ripple of awareness spread throughout her body, and heat settled low in her belly.

If Dax held her hand longer than necessary, Liliana wasn't complaining.

Finally, he released her and took a step backward, his gaze locked with Liliana's.

Liliana couldn't look away.

Amanda clapped her hands. "Now, when the reporters ask about how you two got engaged, you can say he got down on one knee in front of all your friends."

"Now that we have that settled," Carter glanced at his watch, "we need to drive you to the airport. The pilot wanted to get to Riverton and back to Eagle Rock before midnight."

Amanda pushed back from the table and stood. "I do need to get back. I have several appointments tomorrow I don't want to miss."

"When is Hank going to invest in a company jet of his own?" Moe asked.

Stone's lips curved upward. "He's in the process of acquiring an aircraft. He's looking for pilots he can hire on as Brotherhood Protectors. In the meantime, he has access to aircraft that will get us around when we need it."

"It's too bad he can't dedicate a plane to your campaign." Amanda hugged Liliana. "I'd feel better knowing you weren't on those long stretches of highway between towns."

"I need to be closer to the ground," Liliana said. "The people of Wyoming wouldn't understand how I could afford to fly in a private jet and still want to represent them."

She glanced at her own watch and pushed to her feet. "I'm ready to go when you are."

Dax shook his head. "You're not flying back tonight."

Liliana's eyebrows rose up her forehead. "No?"

"No," he said. "We need to spend the evening coming up with our how-we-met story and getting to know more about each other. People will expect us to know a great deal about each other. I suggest we stick as close to the truth as possible to keep it simple and straight."

Liliana nodded. "I'm supposed to be in Cody tomorrow afternoon to greet the people, and in Jackson the following day. Cheyenne's on Friday and Douglas this weekend for the State Fair." She cocked an eyebrow. "Are you sure you're up to all of this? It's a lot of hotels and interaction with people."

Dax gave a single nod. "We can be on the road early tomorrow morning. Between tonight and tomorrow's drive, we should have enough time to learn what we need to know about each other."

Liliana nodded. "Sounds like a plan."

"Do you want to sit in the bar, in the lobby or on the porch?" he asked.

"The porch." Liliana figured it was darker out there. Dax wouldn't be able to see when her cheeks turned red or when she stole glances in his direction.

He nodded. "I'll grab a blanket and meet you out there." Dax left the dining room.

Liliana's gaze followed him, her heart fluttering as she observed his natural swagger.

Amanda leaned into her shoulder. "He's hot, don't you think?"

Heat rose up Liliana's neck, spreading across her cheeks. "I didn't notice," she lied.

Amanda laughed. "Bullshit."

When Dax disappeared around a corner, Liliana hugged Amanda. "You need to go."

"And you need to give yourself permission to flirt."

"He's my bodyguard, not my boyfriend," Liliana whispered.

Amanda shrugged. "Just saying. You've led a celibate life. It's time to get laid and maybe fall in love."

Carter stepped beside Amanda, slipped an arm around her shoulders and kissed her cheek. "Talking about me?"

Amanda grinned up at him. "Absolutely, my love." She winked at Liliana. As she walked away, she said over her shoulder, "Think about it."

Liliana stared at Amanda's retreating figure.

Flirt?

No way. She didn't know how.

Getting laid was out of the question. It would complicate everything.

And there was absolutely no room in her schedule or life for love.

Or was there?

CHAPTER 4

DAX LEFT the dining room and hurried to his room, where he grabbed the throw blanket off his bed. He spun and left the room seconds later, telling himself he needed to hurry because he didn't want to let her out of his sight, and they didn't have much time to get to know each other. Liliana would run the gauntlet of voters and reporters the following afternoon.

Truth was, he was in a hurry to get back to her because she drew him like a magnet. He also worried about leaving her alone for too long, afraid whoever was after her would have discovered where she'd gone.

He left the lodge through the lobby door, stepping out onto the wide back porch lined with rocking chairs and porch swings on either end. At first, he thought she might not have come out yet. When a shadowy silhouette detached itself from one of the brace posts, he knew it was her.

Her tall, lean figure and long straight hair were a dead giveaway. Making his way across the porch, he stopped beside her. "Are you sure it's not too cold for you out here?"

"I'll be fine with the blanket." She tipped her head up, the moonlight glinting in her dark eyes. "Rocking chairs or porch swing?"

"Swing," he said. "We'll be able to share the blanket."

She nodded, crossed to one of the porch swings and sat on one side, leaving enough room for Dax to drop down beside her.

"It's amazing how quickly the temperatures drop after the sun sets," he said as he spread the blanket over her lap and his.

Staring into the darkness, he frowned. "We might be better off inside." He started to rise.

Her hand on his thigh kept him seated. "It's fine. I'm used to the cold air. I grew up not far from here. As children on the rez, we played outside no matter the weather. Besides, the blanket is cozy."

"Well, that's a start." Bracing his foot against the deck, he pushed the swing back a little and raised his foot, letting the chair swing forward. Dax leaned back. "You grew up on the reservation. Mother? Father?"

"My father died in a car accident. He was driving drunk. My mother raised me," she said.

"That couldn't have been easy. A single parent, raising a child is hard enough." He shook his head. "I can't imagine it was any easier on the reservation."

"It wasn't. With unemployment rates high and wages low, she had to work two jobs just for us to survive." Liliana stared at her hands in her lap. "I wanted to help. While other kids were out drinking and raising hell, I buckled down in school earning good grades and scholarships. After high school, I went to college on those scholarships and then to grad school."

"To become a lawyer?" Dax asked.

She nodded. "I worked hard to get where I am today because I wanted to give back to my mother for all her sacrifices." Liliana grew silent.

"And did you?" Dax prompted quietly.

Liliana gave a brief smile that didn't reach her eyes. "My mother died the week before I got my results for the bar exam."

Dax reached for Liliana's hand. "Car wreck?"

Liliana shook her head. "Pneumonia. One minute she had the sniffles and a sore throat. The next minute, she was gasping for breath. They rushed her to the hospital and put her on a ventilator. That didn't help. Her lungs filled with fluid, and she couldn't fight it anymore." A single tear rolled down her cheek. She swiped at the moisture as her cheeks suffused with color. "I didn't mean to be morbid."

"Not at all. As your fiancé, I should know these things."

She wiped away more tears and squared her shoulders. "What about you?" Liliana cocked an eyebrow. "Parents?"

"Just the opposite. Raised by my father. My mother skipped out on us when I was five."

"Wow." Liliana squeezed his hand. "That had to be hard on your father."

"My father could be hard on anyone. He was a Marine, not only at work but at home as well."

Liliana nodded. "A woman who isn't used to the lifestyle could find that intimidating."

Apparently, his mother had been intimidated enough to abandon her husband and young son.

"So, I take it you grew up in a strict environment," she said.

"I did."

"Which made it easy for you to go into the military yourself."

"It did."

Her lips twitched. "As a Marine?"

"No." His eyes narrowed. "I didn't want to go through basic where my father had been a drill instructor for so long, and I had some misguided desire to prove myself on my own, in a different branch of the military. I joined the Navy."

"From what Amanda told me, all the people hired into the Brotherhood Protectors have Special Operations backgrounds. In the Navy, that would mean you became a Navy SEAL?"

He nodded.

"I'm impressed," she said. "I understand the training is very difficult. Not many who start finish. I bet your father was proud."

Dax's hand tightened around hers.

Liliana glanced toward him. "No?"

"He doesn't know."

"What do you mean?"

"He was diagnosed with early-onset Alzheimer's while I was in BUD/S training. It progressed quickly and he's been in a veteran's nursing home ever since."

"I'm so sorry," she whispered, leaning her shoulder against his.

"He can't remember that I'm a grown man, but he remembers a lot of his younger years and enjoys sitting around the break room with other veterans talking about their glory days."

"HOW OFTEN DO YOU SEE HIM?" Liliana asked.

"When I'm in South Carolina for any length of time, I visit often. Otherwise, twice a year." His father's failing health had forced Dax to come to terms with how his father had raised him. Seeing a man who had been so strong, now so weak, mentally and physically, had made Dax realize how quickly life could change.

"Did you ever hear from your mother?" Liliana asked.

The question made his chest tighten. "For years, my father told me she'd died. Her death had been easier for me to understand, especially when I was younger. When he finally told me she'd walked out on us..." He shook his head. "No. I never tried to find her."

Liliana clasped his hands with both of hers and held them for a few silent moments. "Didn't you ever want to hear her side of the story?"

"I couldn't get past her leaving me at five years old with my father." His hand tightened on hers. "The man didn't have a warm bone in his body."

"She might've been so miserable she had to get away or lose herself."

"She left a five-year-old boy with a man who couldn't tell the difference between a boy and a Marine recruit," he bit out, his fists tightening.

"Okay. I get it. You still harbor a lot of resentment toward a woman you don't know." She leaned into him again. "Can you lighten up? You're hurting me."

Immediately, he released her hand and pushed to his feet. "I'm sorry."

Liliana shook her hand as if to get blood flowing

back into her fingers. "It's okay." She patted the seat beside her. "We've only just begun. Shall we bring our discussion back to less contentious topics like our favorite sports teams and who we voted for in the last election?" She smiled up at him.

He stared down at her, his brow furrowing.

"I promise not to bring up your family again." She patted the seat again. "Please. We have to make this charade appear like the real deal, or I'll get slaughtered at the polls."

Her smile made him want to apologize for being so touchy about his mother and father. He wished he hadn't bared his soul. He could have told her they were both dead and left it at that.

What was it about this woman that had made him open up about his upbringing? He'd never told another woman about his childhood or the mother who'd abandoned him. This was an undercover operation. He could have told her anything as long as they stuck to the story.

Dax shook his head. "I'm done for the night. I want to get an early start tomorrow. We have over two hours on the road. That should give us enough time to get our stories straight." And a night's rest would give him time to get his shit together. He was on an assignment to protect this woman from danger.

"Okay. I need to figure out where I'm sleeping tonight."

He held out his hand and pulled her to her feet. "You need to be in the room next to mine."

"I'll get with Mr. Jacobs. Hopefully, that one's available." She walked beside Dax, their shoulders touching as they entered the lobby through the double doors.

"Oh, there you two are." John Jacobs hurried toward them. "I have the key to your room." He held out a key card. "It's next to Dax's."

"You were reading our minds," Liliana said with a smile, taking the key from the older man's hand. "Thank you for dinner and the room. I'm sorry to be a bother and on such short notice."

"You're not a bother," Mr. Jacobs said. "I just wish you weren't being harassed. It's hard enough running for an office without being targeted."

Liliana nodded. "Tell me about it. It's my first time running."

"And I'd venture to guess it's your first time in an explosion." John touched her arm. "You're in good hands with Dax. My boy only works with the best of the best."

Dax's heart warmed. This was the kind of love and affection he'd wished his father had shown him growing up.

Then again, he wouldn't be the man he was had his father not been the uptight asshole he'd been.

Yeah, and he might not have been so distrusting

of all women if his mother hadn't bailed on them when he was so young.

His glance swept over Liliana Lightfeather. She had a way of making people trust her. Her open smile and genuine concern for others could make a man forget the vow he'd made to himself over a decade ago. *Never let a woman steal your heart.* They couldn't be trusted. If a mother could abandon her husband and son, any woman could do the same. Why set himself up for heartache?

Hell, he'd watched so many of his SEAL teammates marry and divorce. His own father had learned his lesson after his wife had walked out on him. He'd never married again.

Dax had learned from his father's failed marriage. He wouldn't let himself fall into the trap only to be proven right. Love was a weakness. His father had taught him never to be weak.

Thankfully, he was a confirmed bachelor, immune to falling in love. He didn't believe in it. Now, lust? That's what it was all about. He didn't deny himself a healthy romp in bed as long as there were no strings attached.

"Oh," John lifted a hand, "Kyla left some clothes in the room for you, seeing as how you didn't bring anything with you. I also stocked the bathroom with toiletries you'll need."

"Thank you," Liliana said. "And be sure to thank Kyla."

"She came here with nothing, like you. She knows how awkward it can be to have only one set of clothes." Mr. Jacobs grinned. "She's since been on a shopping trip for all the essentials. Not that she's all that into fashion. She's good for my Stone. He's met his match with that one."

"I'm happy for them both." Liliana glanced around the lobby. "Which way to the room?"

John Jacobs lifted his chin toward Dax. "Your protector will see you to your room. I'm going to set up the coffeemaker for the morning. Then I'm off to bed. You're welcome to help yourself in the kitchen. There's ham for sandwiches and cocoa if you fancy a cup of hot chocolate before you hit the rack. If I don't catch you before you leave in the morning, good luck with your campaign. The state of Wyoming would be well-represented by you, I'm sure."

"Thank you, Mr. Jacobs." Liliana hugged the man. "Thank you for your support and kindness."

The older man's cheeks turned a ruddy shade of red. "I only speak the truth. We need more people in congress who work for the people, not for the big businesses who are only interested in lining their pockets." He glanced toward Dax. "Take good care of her, you hear?"

"Yes, sir." Dax hooked Liliana's elbow and led her across the lobby toward a hallway. "Our rooms are this way."

"Mr. Jacobs is a generous man."

"Yes, he is. He took us all in when we came back from our stint in Afghanistan. We didn't have jobs or places to stay. All we knew was that we wanted to continue working as a team. Mr. Jacobs' son, Stone, is a good man as well. He has our backs, and we sure as hell have his."

"You're all pretty tight." Liliana walked at his side. "What would you be doing now if you hadn't come to work for Brotherhood Protectors?"

"I don't know," Dax said. "We were all trained to fight and defend. What else could we do in the civilian world?"

"You could work in law enforcement or as a prison guard."

"As a team?" Dax shook his head. "We were lucky Hank Patterson came to our rescue in Afghanistan when the U.S. pulled out before we could get out ourselves. Not only did Hank get us out, but he also offered us a place in his organization, utilizing our skills to benefit others. And we got to stay together as a team. Stone, Bubba, Manning, Hunter and Moe are my brothers."

"You're lucky." She smiled up at him. "I was an only child."

"Something we have in common," he said. "But now, I have brothers on this team and scattered around the world. They drill it into our heads in training to rely on each other, to always have the others' backs." He stopped in front of a door. "This is your room," he said.

"Thank you for taking me on." She slid her key through the card reader and twisted the handle.

Dax touched her arm. "Let me check the room before you go in."

She frowned. "Do you think my attacker followed me here?"

"I doubt it, but I want you and me to be in the habit of always clearing the room before you enter."

She nodded and stepped aside, allowing him to go in first.

The room was small but comfortable, with a queen-sized bed taking up most of the space and a small table with two chairs near the French doors leading out onto a balcony.

He looked in the small wardrobe, under the bed and in the bathroom shower. It was empty of anyone who might feel the need to attack a congressional candidate.

Liliana stood in the doorway until he returned to her.

"All clear. If you need me for anything, I'm in the room beside yours. Let me have your cell phone."

She frowned. "Do I get it back?"

When she held out her cell phone, he didn't take it. "Unlock it," he demanded.

After she'd unlocked it, he took it, added his name and cell phone number to her contacts list and made himself one of her favorites. "If you need anything, or hear anything go bump in the night, call me, text me or bang on the wall. I'll be there."

"This is an old building," she argued. "It will make noises just settling."

"If it concerns you, it concerns me. I'll come." He handed her the phone. "The French door is locked. Shove a chair under the door handle. I'll wait outside your door until I hear the lock click."

"I thought we were safe here." She held up her hand. "I know. I need to get in the habit, and it might as well start here." She gave him a crooked smile. "I'll do everything you suggest."

"Good girl," he said, his lips quirking on the corners. Her crooked smile made his heart beat a little more erratically than he was used to. He chalked it up to leaving her on her own in her room. "Going forward, I'll be staying in your room with you if we can't get a room with connecting doors."

Her brow twisted. "Are you sure it's necessary?"

He nodded. "I can't let you out of my sight and still protect you."

Liliana sighed. "I guess it won't hurt to be extra careful until election day."

"Exactly." He stepped around her and out into the corridor. "Good night, Miss Lightfeather."

"Remember, it's Liliana." She stepped toward him, leaned up on her toes and pressed her lips to his.

He hadn't expected her to kiss him. When she did,

it stunned Dax into silence. Her mouth was soft, her lips full and her hands were on his chest. Electric current raced from everywhere she touched through his body, pooling low in his groin. His cock hardened.

When she stepped back, she shook her head, frowning. "We'll have to make it more convincing than that. Perhaps we should practice an engaged couple's kiss along with memorizing our story." She raised an eyebrow. "Care for a do-over?"

Before he could think of a reason why he shouldn't, he reached out, wrapped his arms around her and pulled her up against his body, molding her form to his.

His fingers weaved into the hair at the back of her neck, and he tugged gently, angling her face upward.

He claimed her mouth in a kiss so hot and demanding he couldn't end it until he was forced to come up for air.

When he released her lips, he continued to hold her around her waist, his arms refusing to let go. "Better?"

Her eyes wide, the pulse beating wildly at the base of her throat, Liliana looked up into his face, her tongue sweeping across her swollen lips. "Y-yes. That should do it." Her voice came out as little more than a breathy whisper. "Thank you."

Liliana continued to stare up into his eyes for another long moment.

Realizing what he'd just done, Dax dropped his arms to his sides. It took a great amount of effort to keep them there when all he wanted to do was take her back into his arms, carry her over the threshold to the bed and make mad, passionate love to her well into the night.

The desire to do just that threatened to overwhelm him.

Dax stared down into her face. She was breathing hard, and her cheeks were flushed. "Go to bed, Liliana, before…"

"Before what?" she whispered. Her tongue swept across her mouth again, making Dax all kinds of crazy.

"Before nothing," he said, his voice a low growl. "Just go."

She frowned. "Did I do something wrong?"

He shook his head. If she didn't go soon, he'd lose his grip on his control and do something they'd both regret in the morning. "Goodnight, Liliana."

He backed her through the doorway, grabbed the handle and pulled it toward him. "Remember to lock the door and block it with the chair."

Pulling the door shut, he leaned his forehead against it until he heard the lock click in place.

If he had to kiss her like that too often, this job was going to be a hell of a lot harder than he'd thought.

He wasn't sure he could remain neutral and unaffected. That kiss…

Wow.

He had his work cut out for him.

The good thing was that he wouldn't have to fake his desire for his fake fiancée. The bad news was that his desire for the pretty congressional candidate was all too real.

CHAPTER 5

LILIANA TOSSED and turned into the night. Every time she closed her eyes, echoes of the explosion blasted through her head. She fought to erase those sounds by thinking of something else.

The only other thing that stood out in her mind and trumped the explosion was Dax pulling her close for that practice kiss. That image took over, raced through her mind and stirred her blood all over again.

How was she going to keep a cool head when the man made her thoroughly aware of him in a very personal way?

She laid a hand across her belly, feeling the burning desire coiling at her core. How long had it been since she'd been with a man?

Liliana sat up in bed and tried to remember.

Too long.

That was it.

She'd gone far too long without sex.

Nothing more.

Could the Brotherhood Protectors have assigned a less...attractive man to provide for her security?

She flopped against the pillow, grabbed the spare pillow and covered her face. Maybe if she smothered herself just a little, she'd pass out and sleep. After a couple of minutes, she realized she could still breathe.

Tossing the pillow aside, she turned onto her side and stared at the starlight shining through the window around the edges of the curtain.

Maybe some fresh air would calm her and allow her to finally go to sleep. The next day would be busy, requiring stamina and endless cheerfulness. She couldn't show up to a campaign rally appearing exhausted, with dark circles beneath her eyes.

"Who am I kidding?" Liliana shoved the blanket aside and climbed out of bed. Quietly, so as not to wake the man in the room beside hers, she moved the chair from beneath the doorknob and opened the French door.

The hinge squeaked. Liliana flinched and strained to hear movement on the other side of the wall. When she didn't hear anything, she stepped out onto the balcony in her borrowed white cotton nightgown that came to mid-thigh and let the cool mountain air wash over her.

"Couldn't sleep, either?" a deep male voice sounded not far from where she stood.

Liliana spun and lowered into the fighting stance she'd learned in Taekwondo.

A dark silhouette moved away from the wall of the building into the glow of starlight.

Her heart still racing, Liliana let go of the breath she'd been holding in a whoosh. "Oh, it's you." She pressed a hand to her wildly beating heart and laughed shakily. "You scared me."

"Luckily, it was only me," he said, crossing the few short steps to join her at the rail. "If your attacker had followed you here, you could have just given him an easy target by stepping out of your room alone...at night."

"Oh, please." She laid her hands on the rail and lifted her face to the night, brightly lit by the millions of stars shining in the crisp, clean mountain air. "I just needed some fresh air to clear my head."

"I get it," he said. "So much has happened over the past twenty-four hours. It's a lot to take in."

"You're probably used to things exploding around you, having been deployed many times," she said.

"I wouldn't say that you get used to it, but you learn to deal with it."

"So many don't learn how to deal with it and end up taking their own lives to end the trauma," Liliana said.

"I don't recommend that. If the explosion is still

keeping you awake or giving you nightmares, talk to someone."

"I'm talking to you," she said softly. Although the explosion was only half of what was keeping her from sleep. The man standing so close to her was the other half.

He moved closer and slipped his arm around her shoulders. "You're going to be okay. I promise."

"I'm not so sure," she said as her knees shook and heat flared like a lit match, landing on dry tinder.

"Are you worried I won't be able to protect you?"

She gave a short sharp laugh. "No, I believe you'll protect me from whoever is trying to attack me."

"Then what else are you afraid of?"

Liliana shook her head. "It's just a feeling." She couldn't tell him she was afraid of herself and the rush of longing she'd experienced when he'd kissed her. The feeling had been so intense that it had shaken her to her very core and threatened to do so again as she stood in the curve of his arm.

He chuckled. "Can you be more specific? I can't help if I don't know what I'm up against."

"Sorry. That's as specific as I can get. Suffice it to say, I'm feeling a bit insecure at the moment and hoped a breath of fresh air would help calm my nerves and let me sleep."

"Fair enough." He stood silently, holding her against him, allowing her to get that breath of fresh air.

The fact he was holding her was doing anything but calm her. No matter how much his touch disturbed her, she couldn't pull away from him.

In fact, it was only an extremely tenuous hold on her control that kept her from turning in his arms and giving herself up for another of his kisses.

They stood for what felt like an eternity or a fleeting second. Liliana's thoughts were such a jumble she couldn't decide which.

When Dax moved, Liliana remembered to breathe, dragging in that cool mountain air she'd come out to claim.

Dax turned her toward him, making her heart thunder against her ribs and her breath hitch in her lungs. Would he kiss her like he had before?

Liliana closed her eyes and lifted her face, ready to accept that kiss and, if things advanced to the next level...so be it.

Dax cupped her cheeks in his palms. "You're entirely too beautiful, Liliana Lightfeather. Go to sleep before I do something we'll both regret." He tipped her face down and pressed his lips to her forehead.

Liliana's eyes opened, disappointment tightening her chest. "I live by the motto of No Regrets," she said, lifting her chin.

"Me, too," he said. "Now, go to bed before we test that motto."

A hair short of begging him to take her, Liliana

drew in a deep breath, turned on her heels and marched back into her bedroom, closing the door behind her with a loud click.

"Lock it," his voice said through the glass window.

If Liliana had held the hope of him following her through the door, his words threw icy water on the fire in her belly. She turned the deadbolt and shoved a chair up against the knob.

He'd have to break down the door, a chair and her anger at being rejected to get into her room now.

She backed away from the door, deep in her heart half-hoping he would do all those things, storm into her room and make mad, passionate love to her.

Only then would she get this crazy longing out of her mind and body. Then they could get on with business—her with her campaign, him with his protection service.

"Oh, and Liliana?"

She rushed to the door and rested her hand on the chair, ready to move it aside. "Yes?"

"Just so you're aware, that gown is practically see-through in the starlight. If you wear it down to breakfast, you might want to cover up with a robe."

Anger flared brighter.

"Thanks," she said, her tone flat.

Her gown was see-through, and she'd all but offered herself to him, which could only mean he was not as into her as she was into him.

Like a balloon with a slow leak, she sank onto the

bed, slipped her legs beneath the covers and laid back on the pillow.

His earlier kiss had only been for practice. It meant no more to him than a stage kiss for the undercover acting they would have to do to convince any onlookers they were truly an engaged couple, happily in love and ready for marriage.

Liliana stared up at the ceiling, shaking her head. "He's not that into you."

Why should she care? She didn't have time in her life for a relationship, even if he was.

Still, it would have been nice to have a fling before getting down to the business of representing her state in congress. Her life wouldn't be her own once she was voted into the office.

She clenched her fists, her jaw hardening. And she would win the vote if it took visiting every town in the state to get the voters to consider her. She was the better candidate.

Liliana closed her eyes and forced air in and out of her lungs at a slow, steady pace. She would sleep and wake refreshed and ready to tackle another day, despite being rejected by her bodyguard.

He was just her bodyguard.

She needed to remember that and get on with her life.

. . .

SHE MUST HAVE FALLEN asleep because the incessant ringing of an alarm jerked her back to consciousness after what felt like a few short minutes since she'd closed her eyes.

Liliana rolled over and hit the stop button on her cell phone alarm to silence the noise.

She closed her eyes and would have fallen back to sleep, but her cell phone vibrated on the nightstand with an incoming call.

Rather than slap the cell phone into the next dimension, she lifted it and answered the call. "Yes?"

"Good morning, sunshine," Dax's deep, male voice sounded in her ear, annoyingly cheerful.

"What's so good about it?" she murmured.

"The sun is shining, there's no rain in the forecast and you're alive to face another dynamic day of campaigning." He paused speaking. "Are you getting up, or do I have to come to get you up?"

She hesitated, the thought of Dax storming into her room more of a temptation than a threat. Hadn't she decided he was just her bodyguard, not a potential fling?

Drawing in a deep breath, she let it out and responded. "I'm up."

"Good. I'll meet you in the hall in five minutes."

"Five minutes? I can't get ready in five minutes."

"Okay, ten. Not a second longer. Get moving, Congresswoman Lightfeather. You have voters to influence. Election day is around the corner."

She groaned. "I'm moving. I'm moving. See ya in ten." Tossing the cell phone onto the nightstand, Liliana groaned and lay back against the pillow.

A knock on the wall made her start.

"I'm moving," she called out and tossed the blankets aside. "Is it too late to get a different bodyguard?" she muttered.

"I heard that," Dax called out. "And yes. It's too late."

Liliana chuckled. Okay, he was a nag and a morning person, but he was nice to look at...as long as she didn't touch.

Hurrying into the bathroom, she washed her face, ran a brush through her hair and pulled it back, twisting it into a long, thick braid. Without her own makeup and a flat iron, she couldn't do much more with her appearance. And she'd be wearing the same outfit as she had the day before.

Which reminded her...

Liliana checked the time. With three minutes to spare, she called her assistant, Rachel.

"Oh, thank god," Rachel answered. "Why didn't you call me last night? I was so worried until Amanda texted me to let me know you'd arrived in West Yellowstone safely."

"I'm sorry. I should've been in touch a lot sooner. A lot has happened, and I'll fill you in when I see you, but first, I need you to do me a favor."

"Anything. You want me to drive out to West Yellowstone? I can be there in two hours."

"No. That won't be necessary. Since Cody has been postponed, I want to get a head start on Jackson. We'll likely get on the road in the next hour. Have you heard from the bomb squad? Is my vehicle safe?"

"Yes. I called the tribal police. They say the bomb squad cleared your car. No explosives were found." Rachel laughed, though the sound wasn't filled with humor. "Sounds funny to say that. Funny, but not funny. Kind of sobering, if you ask me."

"Yeah. I need you to swing by my car, get my overnight bag and the suits I had hanging in the backseat and bring them to Jackson today. Better yet, you can drive my car rather than put miles on yours. We can regroup and go over everything once we get to Jackson."

"Good," Rachel said. "I'm feeling out of the loop with you disappearing to West Yellowstone. Next time you fly off in a private jet, remember me, will ya?"

"You know I will. Before you leave Riverton, could you stop by campaign headquarters and let everyone know I'm all right and thinking about them?"

"Will do."

"I don't know what I'd do without you, Rach. See you in Jackson in about four hours...?"

"You bet," Rachel said and ended the call.

A minute past the ten Dax had given her, Liliana tucked her cell phone into her suit jacket pocket, pulled open her door and dashed through the doorway, slamming into a rock-solid chest.

Hands came around her to steady her.

"Whoa, there," Dax said. "I really didn't expect you to make it out in ten minutes. Are you okay?"

Breathless from close proximity to Dax, Liliana laughed shakily. "I'm fine and a minute late, according to my cell phone. Have you been waiting long?"

He shook his head. "I just stepped out of my room when you came barreling out of yours. Good timing. I smell bacon. Are you hungry?"

As the scent of bacon reached Liliana, her stomach rumbled. "Starving."

"Let's see what Cookie has on the menu this morning."

"Lead the way. I'm still a little turned around."

He offered her his elbow.

Liliana should have ignored it and walked on her own, resisting temptation completely. Instead, she hooked her arm through his and walked with him down the corridor, through the lobby to the lodge's dining room.

A buffet had been arranged at one end of the dining room. Guests served themselves.

Stone greeted them as they entered, handing them

each a plate. "Help yourself and join us at the main table."

After selecting yogurt, fruit and a boiled egg, Liliana poured a small glass of cranberry juice and hurried over to the table where Stone, several other team members and the lodge staff had gathered.

"Good morning, Miss Lightfeather," John Jacobs' booming voice filled the room.

"Good morning, Mr. Jacobs. Please, call me Liliana." She found an empty seat and set her plate and glass down.

Stone held her chair as she sank into it.

Kyla carried her plate to the table and waited as Stone held her chair for her. She leaned up on her toes and pressed a kiss to his lips.

Liliana envied their open display of affection. How wonderful would it be to love someone so completely that showing it was as natural as breathing?

Her own breath caught as Dax settled in the seat beside her, his plate full of heaping helpings of scrambled eggs, bacon and sausage with a side of pancakes. He tucked into the food, washing it down with a full cup of steaming coffee.

Kyla cut into a piece of ham and held it up on the end of her fork. "Swede and I did some digging last night." She popped the ham into her mouth and chewed.

Stone chuckled. "Well, are you going to tell us what you found?"

After she finished chewing, Kyla swallowed. "Your opposing candidates are Ronald Merritt and Brad Benton."

Liliana nodded. "Merritt leans far left and Benton far right."

Kyla nodded. "Benton promises to halt further oil pipelines from crossing into Wyoming. He wants to end coal mining. He's also pushing for green energy and electric cars all the way."

"That's right," Liliana said. "He doesn't quite understand that we're a nation highly dependent on fossil fuels. If we limit our production and transfer of those fuels, we become reliant on foreign sources. Not to mention that some electric plants use coal to generate electricity. Until we make green energy cheaper and more accessible, we need fossil fuels, and why not let the people of Wyoming benefit from the jobs that are part of the pipeline industry? We can route them around the sacred lands and national park."

"Merritt agrees with you," Kyla said.

"And he leans far right," Liliana said. "He's also backed by the oil industry as well as some big land developers."

Kyla nodded. "One developer, Tate Harris, wants the government to allow THEnterprises to build mega-resorts, bordering on public land in Yellowstone National Park and on the edge of Wind River Indian Reservation." Kyla snorted softly. "I use the term *bordering* loosely. The plans show the access to the resort cutting through the national park and WRIR lands."

"That will never happen," Liliana said. "I won't let it."

"If Merritt, the GOP pick, is elected, he'll push for Harris's project to go through," Kyla said.

"Is stopping a land development project from going through enough to warrant the complete elimination of an opposing candidate? In that case, why not take out Benton while he's at it?" Liliana shook her head.

Kyla's lips twisted. "Sweetie, you're more of a threat to Merritt than Benton is, based on the preliminary polls."

Liliana's chest swelled. She'd come a long way from a relative nobody to tying and potentially moving ahead of the incumbent.

"Did you find anything about who might have gotten a hold of C-4 explosives?" Dax asked.

Kyla nodded. "The ATF provided a list of individuals or corporations who have purchased C-4 in the past."

Dax leaned forward. "Is THEnterprises on that list?"

Kyla shook her head. "No, but we haven't narrowed the list down to a manageable level yet.

There are several mining corporations that use C-4 close to Riverton. One is RFR Mining Corporation. The other is Buffalo Mining Corporation. There are others in the state that also purchase C-4 for their mining operations. They have strict guidelines for the use and storage."

"Seems like picking a needle out of a haystack," Liliana said. "Even if we find the source of the C-4, we'd have to find who would have taken it from that source."

"One step at a time," Kyla said. "Swede is rooting through their online systems to check inventory statuses. We'll keep you informed if any companies show signs of misuse of the controlled items."

"The source of that C-4 could prove to be key," Stone said. "And there has to be a connection between where that source is and who would've taken the C-4."

Kyla nodded. "We're working that angle. It might take time."

"Are there any particular cases you tried that might've left someone with a grudge who might want to get back at you for ruining his day?" Stone asked.

Liliana frowned. "There are a number of people who might be disgruntled by the outcomes of some of my cases."

"Names?" Kyla asked, pulling out her cell phone to take notes.

"Jason Monahan," Liliana said. "I shut down his

meth lab and sent him to jail for six years. He's out already on good behavior, from what I understand." She frowned. "There's Nolan Farley, a white supremacist I had sent to jail for a hate crime for an unprovoked assault on a Shoshoni man. He spent three years and was freed a few months ago." She shook her head. "Right off the top of my head, I can't remember the names of the others. I only remember those because I was notified of their recent releases."

Stone gave his fiancée a nod. "You got those?"

She nodded. "We'll work those names as well and any others you come up with."

Stone turned to Dax and Liliana. "Will one protector be enough?"

Liliana nodded. "We'll make it work."

"Just don't take any unnecessary risks," Stone said. "And stay close to Dax at all times."

"I will," Liliana said. "Though, how will he protect me from another explosion?"

Stone grinned. "You're in luck. Hank has his man Kujo on the way with his bomb-sniffing dog Six. They should be here any minute. They can run through wherever you're giving a speech prior to your arrival to check for explosives."

The tightness in Liliana's chest loosened. "That *is* good news. I need to thank Mr. Patterson for all he's doing for me."

"Thank him by winning the election," Stone said.

"Hank and his wife don't ask for anything in return. They just want to help where they can."

"I feel honored their assistance is channeled in my direction."

A commotion at the entrance to the dining room made everyone glance in that direction.

A tall man with black hair and blue eyes entered with a large, sable German Shepherd on a lead.

"Speak of the devil..." Stone stood and met the newcomer as he approached the table. "Kujo, good to see you." He held out his hand and took the other man's in a tight grip. "Thank you for coming so quickly."

"The timing was right. Molly, Sadie and Kate are taking the kids on a train ride to Seattle to visit the aquarium."

Stone frowned. "Shouldn't you have gone?"

Kujo shook his head. "Hank and Chuck went with them. I understand Six and I will be the advance team to clear locations prior to our candidate's speaking events." He glanced around. "Where's our candidate?"

Liliana stood. "That would be me."

Kujo's eyebrows hiked, and he laughed. "I was expecting an older woman."

"Sorry to disappoint." Liliana grinned. "However, if things continue to go like they did yesterday, by the time the election rolls around, I will have aged significantly, especially if we have more explosions. I'm

Liliana Lightfeather, by the way. Nice to meet you... Kujo, is it?"

Kujo stepped forward and shook her hand. "Joseph Kuntz," he said. "You can call me Kujo."

She glanced down at the German Shephard. "And this is?"

"Six."

She frowned. "Six? Like the number?"

Kujo reached down to scratch the dog's ears. "That's right. He was my sixth Military Working Dog."

"And he had your six?" Liliana asked.

"That's right," Kujo said. "Six has had my back since I got him as a pup."

"Thank you for coming all this way and for tagging along with us on my campaign trail. Hopefully, Six won't find anything for us to worry about."

"Though that might disappoint him," Kujo said. "I'd be more than happy for a boring job—meaning no explosives found."

Dax held out his hand. "Daxton Young. Dax for short."

Kujo shook his hand and looked around at the others. "Hank has good things to say about you and the team here."

"We're glad to be here," Stone said. "If not for Hank and the Brotherhood Protectors out of Eagle Rock, Montana, we might still be fighting our way out of Afghanistan."

Kujo rubbed his chin. "That was quite the extraction. Glad it went as well as it did."

Stone grinned. "Us, too.' He nodded toward the buffet. "You and Six should grab some breakfast."

Kujo faced Dax. "What's the plan?"

"We're leaving in fifteen minutes." Dax nodded toward Liliana. "You can follow later if you want to catch up with the Yellowstone operations. The speaking event isn't until tomorrow. We'll have time to run Six through the site in the morning."

"After being on the road for several hours, Six and I would like to stretch our legs and see how the renovations are coming along." He glanced toward the buffet. "Six loves bacon almost as much as I do. We didn't have time to eat before we left at zero-dark-thirty."

"Please, grab some chow and join us," John Jacobs said. "I'll get a pot of coffee and a mug for you."

"I'm finished here if you want to get on the road," Liliana said. "I looked at the route to Jackson. The shortest way is through Idaho. I'd rather take the longer route through Wyoming if you don't mind, but it'll add an hour to the trip."

"We have all day to get to Jackson," Dax said. "We're not in a hurry."

"Good. We'll be driving past Yellowstone and the Grand Tetons, some of the most beautiful areas in the country. Makes me proud to be from Wyoming."

"Sounds like a nice drive," Kyla said.

"Hopefully, an uneventful one," Carter said.

"Yeah, but if you get in a pinch, give us a yell," Falcon said. "Wouldn't mind a trip through the parks myself."

Liliana and Dax left the others at the table and headed back to their rooms.

"I just need to brush my teeth, and I'll be ready," Liliana said. "I assume we're riding in your vehicle since mine is back in Riverton...?"

Dax nodded. "We'll go in my truck. It'll be its first big road trip since I bought it."

"A new truck, huh?" she said.

"Yeah, I sold everything before I left for Afghanistan, fully expecting the job to last more than a year," Dax said. "I saw no use in keeping furniture and a vehicle in storage if they weren't going to be used."

"You're starting over, then." Liliana shook her head. "As poor as I was growing up, I always knew I had a home to go to on the reservation. If my family wasn't there, other people I knew and grew up with would take me in and be there for me. I don't know what it's like to be completely rootless."

Dax's lips pressed into a tight line. "As a Navy SEAL, you get used to it. Until you don't. Then it's time to get out and plant some roots of your own. After our stint as mercenaries in Afghanistan, I was ready to find a place to call home."

"And have you found it?"

He shrugged. "I've found a career. As for a home, not yet. That's a work in progress."

"Have you considered Wyoming?"

He laughed. "The entire state?"

"Or somewhere inside the state." Liliana's cheeks heated. "It's a beautiful place to live. Or are you tied to West Yellowstone since that's where your team is located?"

"I think we can live where we want as long as we can get together when needed." Dax stopped in front of her door.

Liliana ran her key card through the scanner and pushed open the door. She waved him inside. "After you."

"Good. You remembered."

"I might not have been trained in the military, but I learn quickly." She grinned as he entered her room first and made a quick pass.

When he came back to where she was standing, he nodded. "All clear."

"Thank you." She looked up into his eyes. "I'm glad you're going with me. I feel safer with you around."

His gaze met hers and held. "I'm glad I'm going as well. And I'm glad Kujo and Six will be ahead of us at the sites. I can protect you from actual, physical attacks, but bombs... That's where Six will earn his pay in treats."

"Let's hope for an uneventful campaign tour," Liliana said.

For another long moment, Dax stood before her. "I have the feeling that nothing about being on a campaign tour with you will be uneventful. And I don't mean that in a bad way." He bent and brushed his lips across hers.

When his head came up, Liliana stared, transfixed, her heart fluttering, her knees going weak. "Practice makes perfect?"

He grinned. "Damn right."

CHAPTER 6

"Favorite color?" An hour and a half down the road, getting close to Yellowstone National Park, Dax had been drilling Liliana, learning more about her life, her preferences and her favorite sports teams.

"Blue," she answered. "Like the big skies over the rez. And you?"

"Green," he answered. "I like when the winter morphs into spring and everything turns green again. It's like a fresh start."

"I like that," she said. "I love spring and the different shades of green."

"To summarize what we've learned so far," Dax said, "your favorite color is blue. You're a dog person, but you like cats, too. Your favorite food is lasagna, you prefer mountains over beaches, you love to travel but love to come home and your favorite sports team is the Denver Broncos."

"You get an A+ for memorization." Liliana laughed. "Let's see if I'm as successful..." She tapped a finger to her chin. "Your favorite color is green, your favorite food is Mexican, you prefer beaches over mountains, you love to travel and don't have a home...which is sad. I can't imagine not having a home. And your favorite sports team is the Patriots."

"Okay, where did we meet?" he asked.

"Easy, at the Grand Yellowstone Lodge. When is a little trickier." She frowned. "Amanda and I went to West Yellowstone six months ago. We met then and have been corresponding since and have met in Cheyenne and Bozeman on different occasions. Your work kept you from visiting me in Riverton if anyone asks."

"Sounds good."

"I'd like to stop at the Yellowstone visitor's center if you don't mind the detour," Liliana said. "The park is such a big draw to our state I'd be remiss in passing it by without stopping."

"We have time, and I've always wanted to visit."

Her eyes widened. "You've never been to Yellowstone?"

He shook his head. "Never came this close to it before now."

"Oh, man. You're in for a treat. We're going to Yellowstone."

He laughed, his chest swelling at her excitement to show off her state's number one destination.

"Do you realize Yellowstone is the first national park in the United States?" she asked.

"Yes. I did know that," he said with a grin. "Stone told me. Even though he grew up in West Yellowstone, Montana, he's proud to be so close to Yellowstone National Park. It was his playground in his youth."

"It's truly magnificent," Liliana said. "A park worth keeping in its natural state.

"Don't you need reservations to get into the park?"

She shook her head. "No. We will need a park pass, though. I had one in my SUV, but that's in Riverton."

"That's okay. I don't mind buying a park pass to see Yellowstone."

"Now we can say our first trip together was to see Yellowstone National Park." Liliana sat back in her seat, her face wreathed in a smile. "You're going to love it."

"I already do." Just because it made her so happy to share it with him made him love the park, sight unseen. Of course, he'd seen pictures of the park's attractions. But to go in person with someone equally excited to be there was a bonus.

His father had never taken the time to travel much with Dax. He'd taken him to the South Carolina beaches a couple of times because they'd been close by.

When Dax had gotten his driver's license, any trips with his father ended. He'd worked hard to save for a banger of a car to get back and forth to an after-school job. He'd saved more and traded up to a four-wheel-drive pickup. He and his friend had spent many days off and nights on the beach, fishing, crabbing and partying.

His real traveling began when he joined the Navy and then the Navy SEALs.

Then he'd gone overseas to posh places like Iraq, Syria, Somalia, and other choice locations requiring their skills. Occasionally, their flights there or back had included stops in Germany, Italy, Australia and other places, giving them enough time to do a little exploring. He hadn't seen much of the interior States like Wyoming, Montana and the Dakotas.

He paid for the park pass and parked at the visitors' center. From there, they explored many of the spitting, spewing, bubbling and oozing geysers, viewed colorful pools and stopped at the visitors center with fifteen minutes to spare before Ol' Faithful's eruption.

While Liliana explored the handcrafts and souvenirs, Dax stood next to the jewelry counter, enjoying watching Liliana's excitement and happiness at visiting her state's pride and joy.

When he turned his head, he noticed a display case of shiny rings. One, in particular, caught his eye. The ring was a simple band in the shape of a mountain with diamond chips along the band. With one eye out for Liliana, he asked the clerk to show him the ring.

"You can get it in sterling silver with rhinestones or white, 14kt gold with real diamonds," she said.

"Show me the one in white gold with diamonds."

The ring was perfect. "I'll take it."

She pulled one out of the display case. "Is there a size you had in mind?" she asked.

"Yes, a size that would fit my fiancée," he turned to find Liliana standing beside him. "Lili, honey, tell this nice young lady what size ring you wear."

"Huh?"

"What size ring do you wear?" the clerk asked. "If you don't know, I have a size set you can use to figure it out."

"I don't know." A frown pulled at Liliana's brow. When the clerk went to find the sizing rings, Liliana leaned close to Dax. "What are you doing?"

"We're engaged. I'm getting you that ring."

She glanced down at the mountain-shaped ring, and her eyes widened. "Oh my God, I love it."

His chest swelled at the look of wonder on her face. "My mountains."

The clerk returned, had her try the fitting rings, selected a size and found the corresponding ring size to fit Liliana's finger.

"Do you want me to wrap it?" she asked.

Dax and Liliana both shook their heads.

"No, she'll wear it out." Dax paid for the ring. When the clerk started to hand the box to Liliana, Dax took it from her, extracted the ring and got down on his knee.

Liliana's cheeks flushed a bright pink. "You don't have to do it again."

"I didn't do it right the first time." He looked up at her.

A crowd gathered around, excited to witness a proposal.

"No, wait." Dax rose to his feet. "What time is it?"

The clerk glanced at the clock on the wall, her eyes widened and a smile spread across her face. "You have exactly 2 minutes to get outside."

Dax grabbed Liliana's hand. "Hurry!" They ran through the store and out to the viewing area in time to see the first puffs of steam rising from Ol' Faithful.

Dropping to one knee, Dax held out the ring. "Liliana Lightfeather, will you marry me?"

Ol' Faithful blew, steam and water rising high into the air.

Liliana laughed and cried, "Yes!" her voice in tune with the geyser's crescendo.

Dax slipped the ring on her finger.

Liliana flung her arms around his neck and they kissed like any real couple in love and getting engaged.

Dax crushed her to him, deepening the kiss until they both were breathless and came up for air. When he looked around, a crowd had gathered, videoing them along with the geyser's eruption.

A young woman approached him. "Would you like me to send you the video of your proposal?"

"Yes," he said, working with the woman to airdrop the video onto his phone, all the while keeping an arm firmly around Liliana's waist.

When Ol' Faithful went back to sleep, in wait for its next showing, Dax and Liliana walked back to his truck in silence.

Once inside the cab, Dax glanced over at Liliana.

She was staring down at the ring on her hand, tears welling in her eyes.

Dax's gut knotted. "What's wrong?"

"Nothing," she said, her voice choking on a sob.

"You're crying," he said, frowning. "Something must be wrong. Do you hate the ring?"

She shook her head, tears streaming down her cheeks. "No, I love it so much. It's just a shame…"

"What's a shame?" He reached across the console and cupped her cheek, his heart squeezing hard in his chest. "Don't cry."

"It's just such a beautiful ring and the perfect setting and perfect proposal. It's a shame it wasn't real." She gave him a weak, watery smile. "You put on a great show. And got the video as well. You're playing this part so well." Her gaze dropped to the ring again.

"You needed a ring. Like Kyla said, people will ask to see the ring."

She nodded. "You're right. I can reimburse you for the cost of the ring."

He shook his head, a surge of anger rising in his throat. "No. It's a gift."

"But I can't accept it."

"You already did. I don't want to discuss it further." His tone was sharp, cutting.

Liliana didn't argue but sat silently as they drove through the park and out the other side into the Grand Tetons.

By then, neither one wanted to stop and admire the view.

Liliana was right. The proposal, the acceptance had all been for show. It wasn't real.

Then why did it feel real? And why was he mad? It was as if he was angry that it wasn't real.

Which was ludicrous. He wasn't the kind of guy who would ever marry.

But if you did...Liliana would be your perfect match.

Again. Ludicrous. She was an attorney on her way to becoming a congresswoman. She'd be in Washington, D.C., representing her state, making laws, passing bills and being an asset to her country. A relationship with a woman like that would require a man of equal standing. Not a washed-up Navy SEAL who only knew how to shoot things.

"What's wrong?" Liliana asked softly.

Dax pulled himself out of his self-defeating musings and shot a glance her way. "Why do you think anything is wrong?"

"You're frowning like someone just shot your dog." Her lips quirked upward. "What were you thinking about?"

For a moment, he paused. "I was thinking people might not buy our charade."

Her brow dipped. "Why not?"

He stared straight out the front windshield at the curving road ahead. "Why would a hot-shot attorney, on her way up the political food chain, marry a former Navy SEAL, who only finished an undergraduate degree in political science? You are in an entirely different league."

Liliana snorted. "Wow. I might have a license to practice law, but I came from the rez. I will never forget that. I learned at an early age that no one is better than anyone else. It's what you do with what you have that makes you special. You have amazing skills and have accomplished so much more, mentally and physically, than only a small fraction of people has succeeded at. I could never do what you've done."

"Still, once you're elected, you'll be off to the nation's capital to help guide our country by passing laws and bills. That's big stuff. Important stuff. I'd be considered a house husband to your political standing. Why would anyone think I was a good match for you?"

She blinked. "Don't be a snob about politicians. Not all politicians are in it for financial and social standing. I really do want the best for my state and the people who live there. I'm running on a platform that emphasizes representing the people, not the big businesses. They'll be even more inclined to think we're a good match because you aren't a politician. You're a Navy SEAL, for Pete's sake."

"Not everyone is impressed by Navy SEALs. Some don't even know what they are."

She rolled her eyes. "Everyone has seen the movies and television specials about Navy SEALs. They know what they represent—and what's not to love about a military war hero?"

"A military war hero turned house husband to the congresswoman."

She laughed. "I can't begin to picture you in an apron, dusting the fine dinner settings." Liliana reached out and touched his arm. "You won't be a house husband because you'll be working for the Brotherhood Protectors, helping others trapped in bad situations. Or, better yet, you'll be in charge of my personal security detail, should I need one."

"When you run for president, you'll need one."

Liliana smiled and leaned her head back against the headrest. "One step at a time. Congress first, ruler of the world next."

He glanced her way, liking the way her lips curled

naturally in a smile and the blue-black sheen of her hair. A man with less baggage than himself could easily fall in love with this woman. "You could do so much better than me."

She turned in her seat, her brow wrinkled. "Are you kidding me? Have you looked in a mirror lately? You're hot! I'll be beating off the women with a stick. If anything, you could do better than a girl from the rez."

He chuckled. "Now, who's the snob? Look at all you've accomplished in such a short amount of time. And you're running for an office at the federal level."

"Some would think that I'm foolish even to try. I'm a woman, a Native American and too young to be a legislator. The odds are stacked against me."

"Yet the polls are favoring you. They must see something in you the other candidates don't have, like integrity, honor and commitment."

"All the same values inherent in the Navy SEALs." She lifted her chin. "Let's agree that we both have merit and let it lie. You're an asset to my campaign, not only as my protector but as my potential partner, my better half."

"I'll do my best to live up to your standard."

"You don't have to work at it. You're way above the bar and more of a good man than most of the men in congress today. How many of them went through the training you did and fought the battles you and your team fought?" She shook her head. "I'm proud to call you my fiancé. Even if it's only for show."

"I couldn't ask for a smarter or more beautiful fiancée," he said.

She gave him a crooked smile. "You're getting good at the role play."

"If you stick close to the truth, it makes it easier." He grinned. "You are beautiful and smart."

She stared out the window, her lips twisting. "All this subterfuge is crazy and messed up. I hope we lure my attacker out into the open. I can handle snakes that I can see. It's the ones in the grass that worry me."

"Agreed." Dax reached out and took her hand. "Promise me you'll stay close to me at all times."

She squeezed his hand. "I promise. I'd like to make it to election day intact."

Dax would like her to make it further than election day. The woman had the ambition and desire to help the residents of her state. He hoped she got that chance. Dax would do his darnedest to make sure she did.

CHAPTER 7

As THEY PULLED into the small town of Jackson, Wyoming, the sun had just ducked below the horizon.

"One of my contributors is putting us up in a ski resort. We'll have a fundraising dinner there tomorrow night where I'll give a speech."

"So, we're free until the dinner tomorrow night?"

Liliana shook her head. "I want to spend the day meeting the people who work in the resorts, not the owners. They're voters, too. Though they didn't contribute to my campaign, I need their votes. They need to know I'm not in the pockets of the wealthy. I'll represent them as much, if not more so, than those who can afford to buy their way into Washington."

"And every vote counts." Dax turned onto the road leading to the resort perched halfway up a mountain. "I'm sure the workers outnumber the owners."

She nodded. "By a long shot."

Dax pulled into the unloading zone in front of the resort and shifted into park.

He got out and rounded the front of the truck to the passenger side.

A porter was there before him, opening Liliana's door. "Will you be checking in?"

Liliana nodded.

"What name is on the reservation?" he asked.

"Lightfeather."

The porter's eyes rounded. He turned and snapped his fingers at the valet standing nearby.

The porter took Dax's duffel bag from the back seat, and a valet asked for his keys.

Dax cupped Liliana's elbow and stepped onto the walkway leading into the building.

"Miss Lightfeather, the manager will see to your needs."

A man dressed in a black suit and red tie, with a gold name badge proclaiming him as the manager, hurried toward them. "Miss Lightfeather, we're delighted to have you stay at our establishment. Please, follow me. You'll be staying in the presidential suite, courtesy of the owners." He handed her his business card. "If you need anything during your stay, all you have to do is call me, 24/7. I'll answer and make sure we satisfy your every desire."

"Thank you," Liliana looked around. "I don't suppose my assistant, Rachel Swain, has arrived…?"

Before the manager could answer, a woman's voice called out, "Lili, there you are!"

Dax turned to find a woman hurrying toward Liliana, rolling a silver, hard-sided suitcase.

She didn't slow as she neared.

For all Dax knew, she could be an overzealous fan or a saboteur with a suitcase full of explosives. Dax didn't know the woman and didn't trust anyone, no matter how normal she might appear. He stepped between the woman and Liliana.

Liliana touched his arm. "It's okay, Dax. Rachel's my assistant."

His eyes narrowed. Dax wasn't convinced the woman wasn't planning on killing Liliana. "What's in the suitcase?"

"My clothes, makeup and toiletries." Liliana stepped past him and grabbed the suitcase handle. "Thank you so much for bringing my things. I didn't relish going to tomorrow's formal function in a scuffed skirt suit."

Rachel frowned. "You are quite the mess, aren't you? Do you hurt anywhere in particular?"

Liliana nodded. "I'm fine. My pride took more of a beating than my body."

Rachel turned to Dax, though her words were for Liliana. "Aren't you going to introduce me to your fella?"

Liliana laughed, the sound dying too quickly. "Rachel...this is Daxton Young...my fiancé."

"What?" Rachel exclaimed. "Your fiancé?"

Liliana nodded, her cheeks flushing dark pink. "My fiancé," she repeated with more conviction and held up her left hand.

Rachel squealed, grabbed her hand and stared down at the mountain ring. "What? When? How did I not know about something as important as a boyfriend and potential husband? This changes so much." She took Liliana's arm and steered her through the lobby to the elevators. "Girl, we need to talk, and you need to spill all the details."

"Don't we need to check in?" Liliana asked.

Rachel held up two keycards. "Done. Let's get up to your suite. I have some news, and I'm sure you two have some as well." She punched the button on the elevator and waited for the doors to open. Once the door opened, Rachel, Liliana and Dax entered the elevator and rode the car up to the top floor where they opened the door to the penthouse suite.

Dax stepped through first. "Stay here until I clear the area."

Rachel shot a glance at Liliana. "I like the way he thinks."

Dax moved through the rooms one at a time checking all the places someone could hide. He returned a couple minutes later. "All clear. You can come in."

Once inside, Rachel closed the door and turned to face Liliana and Dax. "I talked to the police after you left Riverton. They reviewed footage from some of the businesses close to the Blue Moose Tavern. They identified the person who sabotaged the stage in Riverton."

"Yeah?" Dax shot a glance in Liliana's direction. "Who was it?"

Rachel's eyes narrowed. "Jason Monahan. Didn't you recently receive notice he'd been released from prison?"

Liliana nodded.

Dax frowned. "Is Monahan someone you sent to jail?"

Liliana nodded again. "Yes."

"What did they see in the footage to make them think this guy set the charges?" Dax asked.

"He carried a backpack toward the stage a couple of hours before the event. They didn't put it all together until ATF showed up, shortly after you two left. They found the remains of the black backpack, dusted for prints, got enough of a match and tracked Jason to his mobile home."

"Wow," Liliana shook her head. "That was faster than I would've expected.

Rachel grinned. "The good news is, an agent with a trained bomb-sniffing dog came with them. The dog went through the entire mobile home and laid next to a hidden compartment in the back of a closet."

Liliana gasped. "He had more?"

Rachel nodded. "Jason had enough C-4, fuses and detonators to blow up half of the state."

Liliana's brow knitted. "You'd think time in jail would've straightened him out."

"It's like you suspected," Dax said. "He's probably bent on revenge since you put him in jail."

"Do they know where he got the C-4?" Liliana asked.

"They traced the unused C-4 to a mining company outside of Gillette," Rachel said. "Apparently, they had a break-in a few nights ago and had yet to report it. They were scrambling to identify what all was missing."

Liliana snorted. "Now, they know. We're fortunate.

"Do they have security footage of their storage facility?" Dax asked.

Rachel nodded. "There was more than one man involved in the break-in. Both wore black ski masks and gloves. No prints were left."

"Monahan had an accomplice who could have more explosives stashed away," Dax said. "Is he talking? Has he told them who the other guy is?"

Liliana's assistant shook her head. "He lawyered up as soon as they apprehended him. They took him to Cheyenne for questioning and to lock him up. I'll check back with the state criminal investigation team tomorrow to see if they got him to name the other man involved."

"Thank you for being on top of it." Liliana hugged her assistant. "I feel like I fell off the face of the earth after the explosion."

"It might be just as well that you got out of town, and no one knew where you were going," Rachel said. "If someone is still bent on putting you out of the race, they'll follow your schedule."

Liliana smiled across the room at Dax. "Dax is a highly trained combat veteran. He's promised to protect me."

"Good," Rachel said. "I was going to suggest you hire a bodyguard. Having Dax around will be even better. He'll be with you at all times."

"And he's got a friend with a retired Military Working Dog trained in bomb-sniffing." Liliana sighed. "I hate that we have to worry about explosives, but I'm glad he's coming. I don't want any bystanders injured just because they came to hear me speak. Joseph Kuntz and his dog will be here later this evening and will make a pass through the banquet hall tomorrow before the event begins. We'll want to make sure he has accommodations."

Rachel made a note on her smartphone. "I'll get with the resort manager and make it happen. It'll put my mind at rest, knowing the room is clear. Are you still going to conduct your meet-n-greet in town tomorrow morning?"

Liliana nodded. "I think it's important to the working class to know I'm there for them, no matter who threatens me."

Rachel frowned. "Are you sure you'll be safe?"

"I can't campaign if I can't get out and talk to the people."

"Could we at least wrap you in bubble wrap or an armor-plated vest?" Rachel's lips twisted. "When you're out among the people, you're exposed to any nutcase who thinks he can take a shot at you."

"I don't like being a target. It puts others at risk for collateral damage, but I can't let whoever is after me win. I refuse to die and won't concede this election until all the votes are in."

"You have to make it past election day and then some," Dax's jaw hardened. "However, I do like the idea of you wearing an armor-plated vest."

Before he finished his sentence, Liliana was shaking her head. "I'm not going to bulk up with armor plating when the people around me have none." She drew in a deep breath. "God, I hope innocents aren't hurt. Is it wrong of me to keep campaigning? I could be putting others at risk. Sounds selfish to me."

"We don't know what else this person will do to get to you," Rachel said. "You can't step back from your campaign now. You'll lose momentum."

"But am I thinking of the people or my own career?"

Rachel gripped her arms and stared straight into Liliana's eyes. "You are the best candidate and will do great things for the people of our state. But you can't if you're not in a position where you can help. Hiding out in a bunker and losing the election will accomplish nothing."

"She's right," Dax said. "You can't quit now." He liked how Liliana's assistant helped her boss to maintain focus on the prize. The woman cared about her and wanted her to be successful.

Liliana nodded. "No, I can't." She lifted her chin and squared her shoulders. "I'm in this fight to win it."

Rachel stepped back and let her hands fall to her sides. "That's my girl. Now, get cleaned up and dressed in something that hasn't been in an explosion. We'll have dinner in the resort restaurant. You'll want an early start tomorrow to hit the favorite breakfast spot in town when all the locals come in for a bite to eat. I've already got the recommendations."

Liliana smiled at her friend and assistant. "I'm not sure what I'd do without you."

Rachel smiled. "Hopefully, you won't have to find out. I'm headed to the dining room to secure a table for us. See you in twenty minutes? Will that be enough time?"

Liliana nodded.

Rachel faced Dax. "I assume you'll be staying in the suite with Liliana." It was a statement, not a question.

Dax nodded.

"Good. That saves me from having to find another room. I'll work on getting the dog handler and his dog a room as close to you as possible, although it won't be on the top floor."

"Thank you, Ms. Swain," Dax said.

"Oh, please. Call me Rachel. When you two marry, we'll practically be family. Oh, and do you have a suit you can wear? Dining here is pretty formal, and you'll definitely need the suit for the formal event tomorrow night."

"I have one in my duffel bag," Dax said.

Rachel's eyebrows rose. "I'll have housekeeping collect it and press it tomorrow morning. Trousers and a button-up shirt will do for tonight. The suit would be even better."

Liliana laughed. "Rachel keeps me in line, too. She has excellent fashion sense and social timing."

"Nonsense," Rachel flung over her shoulder as she headed for the door. With her hand on the door handle, she glanced over her shoulder. "You're perfectly capable of dressing yourself." Her gaze shifted to Dax with a teasing grin. "Jury's still out on your fiancé. I'm betting he can't even match his own socks." She cocked an eyebrow. "The challenge is on, pretty boy. Prove me wrong."

Dax laughed as Rachel sailed through the door. "Is she always so pushy?" he asked.

Liliana's gaze was on the door through which Rachel had disappeared. "Always. She gets things done."

"An asset to any team."

"Exactly." Liliana crossed to her suitcase, rolled it into the bedroom and lifted it onto the end of the bed.

Dax stood in the sitting room, watching her every move through the open bedroom door.

From the suitcase, Liliana removed a black dress, shoes, matching lace panties and a toiletries kit.

"I've been thinking about our sleeping arrangements," he said.

Her head whipped around, her gaze landing on his. "I didn't even think about that. Is this the only bedroom in the suite?"

"It is." He crossed to the sofa and sat on one of the cushions. It was firm but better than a foxhole, and he could see the door to the room and the entrance to the bedroom. He stood. "I can sleep out here tonight."

Liliana walked out into the sitting room, still holding the dress. "Are you sure? I could sleep on the sofa, and *you* could have the bed."

He shook his head. "That would put you between an intruder and me. Besides, I'm the hired help; you're the celebrity."

She laughed. "Hardly a celebrity."

"Okay, the candidate. The resort gave you the Presidential Suite, not me. You need to be comfortable. You're on tomorrow and need your rest."

Liliana crossed her arms over her chest, dress and all. "And you're protecting me tomorrow and need your rest."

He chuckled. "You'll make a good congresswoman."

Her brow wrinkled. "Why do you say that?"

"You're always concerned about others over your own health and welfare." He touched her cheek. "I hope the voters see how special you are."

She stared up into his eyes, hers so dark and mysterious. Her chin tilted upward, her eyelids sinking low.

Dax leaned closer. With only a few inches between them, all he had to do was tip his head downward to claim her full, rosy lips.

He lowered his head until his mouth was no more than a breath away from hers.

Liliana leaned up on her toes, making the connection complete.

Dax wrapped his arms around her waist and pulled her body against his, deepening the kiss and sweeping past her teeth to caress her tongue.

With her hands resting against his chest, her fingers curled into his shirt, holding him close.

Fire burned inside, his blood burning through his

veins and pooling in his groin.

A soft moan sounded in Liliana's throat, spurring Dax's desire into a blazing inferno.

A knock on the door barely broke through the haze of lust fogging his brain. He lifted his head.

When the knock sounded again, he stepped back, releasing his hold on her body.

Liliana swayed toward him and then straightened. She touched her fingers to her swollen lips and stared at him.

"Someone's at the door," he said.

She nodded.

He bent to scoop up the dress she'd dropped and handed it to her. An electric charge shot through his system when their hands touched. It was all he could do to keep from taking her into his arms again.

Dax turned away from Liliana, wondering what the hell he thought he was doing. The woman was a congressional candidate. He was her bodyguard, not her real fiancé or lover. He had no business kissing her as he'd done.

But, sweet Jesus, it had felt so good.

He crossed to the door and checked through the peephole.

Rachel stood on the other side, her hand raised, ready to knock again.

Dax opened the door before her knuckles touched the wooden panel. "Yes, ma'am."

She smiled up at him. "Just wanted to let you

know that your dog handler arrived and is in a room directly below yours. I invited him to have dinner with us."

"Thank you for letting us know."

She looked past Dax to Rachel. "Do you want me to have that dress pressed for you?"

Liliana shook her head. "No, thank you. I can manage."

Rachel nodded. "I'm available tonight if you want to practice your speech."

"Thank you, Rachel," Liliana said.

Rachel's brow dipped. Her gaze shifted from Liliana to Dax and back to her boss. "If you need me for anything, shoot me a text. Otherwise, I'll leave you two lovebirds alone." She winked and turned away with a grin.

Dax closed the door, squared his shoulders and faced Liliana. "I'm sorry. That won't happen again." He stopped himself short of saying, *Unless you want it to.* He wanted to kiss her again more than he wanted to take his next breath.

"Right," she said. "We should save it for the public." Her cheeks flushed a soft pink as she returned to the bedroom and closed the door between them.

Dax should have been glad for the barrier, but his gut knotted. He felt as if he'd lost something. How could he have lost something he'd never had in the first place?

CHAPTER 8

LILIANA SHOWERED, dried her hair and ironed her dress, her mind rolling over and over that kiss. Where had that come from? What had made him lean down and her rise up to meet him? They barely knew each other. Well, other than what they'd talked about on the drive down. Still, they really didn't *know* each other.

Oh, but they had chemistry.

No doubt.

But was chemistry enough, considering everything stacked against them?

Whatever was between them, she couldn't lose herself so completely like she had as soon as his lips had touched hers.

After she applied a light amount of makeup, she slipped into the dress and the high heels that matched and then studied her reflection in the mirror.

Her lips were still slightly swollen from the incredible kiss she'd shared with Dax. She raised her hand to touch her fingertips to her mouth, still tingling from his.

How could she face him when all she wanted to do was kiss him again?

Truthfully, that wasn't *all* she wanted to do to him, but it was enough to make her shy and hesitant when she opened the bedroom door.

He stood at the window, overlooking the mountain, his broad shoulders, narrow hips and muscular thighs making her heart race. He still wore the same clothes he'd worn earlier. Draped over the back of the sofa were a black suit and white shirt. He turned.

"The bathroom is all yours," she said. "I left the ironing board up if you'd like me to iron your suit while you're getting ready."

He turned to face her, his gaze sweeping over her from head to toe, his eyes flaring. "Wow," he said. "You clean up beautifully."

Her cheeks heated. "I'm sorry I took so long."

"Don't be sorry. The time was well-spent." He smiled. "You're gorgeous."

Liliana didn't think her cheeks could get hotter. She must be beet-red by now. Very unflattering. "Thank you."

She left the doorway, walked to the mini bar and found a bottle of red wine.

Dax gathered his toiletries, suit and dress shoes and entered the bedroom, calling out over his shoulder, "I won't be long."

"I'm not in a hurry. I need to go over my speech for tomorrow."

He turned around. "I'd be happy to listen if you'd like."

"Thanks," she said. "I've given most of this before. I just need to review and remember the words I want them to hear most. I believe every word and know them deep in my heart. I just don't want to say them wrong and have someone misquote me."

He nodded. "The media can be ruthless."

"Yes, they can. They can also be helpful."

"If they're on your side," he finished.

"True."

"Ten minutes, tops," he said and entered the bathroom, closing the door behind him.

Liliana found herself straining to hear the sound of the water going on in the shower. Her imagination took flight with thoughts of Dax standing beneath the spray, naked, wet and so very tempting.

Her pulse sped and heat burned at her core. She poured herself a glass of wine and carried it to the window. Though it was dark outside, the stars shone on the mountain, bathing it in a blue glow.

The wine and the view helped to calm her raging libido. By the time Dax emerged from the bathroom, she was almost back to her cool, collected self.

Then he stepped out into the living room, dressed in the neatly pressed black suit, his damp hair slicked back and more handsome than a man had a right to be.

"Wow," she said. "You clean up well."

He chuckled. "Thank you."

"Do you have much call for a black suit as a protector?" she asked, taking a sip of her wine, enjoying the warmth spreading through her body. She blamed it on the wine though she knew better. Dax made her warm all over.

His smile faded. "I bought this suit after I got out of the Navy. I've only worn it to funerals."

"Oh," she said. "That's incredibly sad."

He nodded. "But tonight, the suit gets a break. It gets to celebrate going out with a beautiful woman." Dax held out his arm. "Shall we?"

Liliana hooked her arm through his, shrugging away the image of the funerals the suit had been to. "I don't know about you, but I'm hungry."

"Me, too."

"The resort has one of the best chefs in all of Wyoming and most of the west coast."

"Great. Hopefully, he serves man-sized portions."

Liliana laughed. "Man-sized portions?"

"Not the dainty bites they serve at fancy restaurants for insane prices." He opened the door, checked the hallway and led her to the elevator.

"I'm sure we can ask for more if you don't get enough." Her heart lighter, she stepped onto the elevator with the mirrored walls, thinking what a great-looking couple they made. They even looked happy, like a newly engaged pair should.

Too bad it was all just pretend.

That thought put a little damper on her mood as she rode the elevator down to the restaurant level and stepped out.

As they approached the restaurant doors, the hotel manager was there to greet them. "Your table is ready, Miss Lightfeather."

"Thank you."

He led the way to a table near the back of the room, away from the swinging door to the kitchen.

Rachel was there, seated beside a man with black hair and blue eyes. Lying on the floor beside him was a sable German Shepherd, patiently waiting for his person's next command.

Rachel leaped to her feet. "There you are." She turned to the man who'd risen from his chair. "I've been getting acquainted with Mr. Kuntz and his dog, Six." She smiled at the pair. "Did you know Six served in Afghanistan for three years? He saved so many lives in his work." She laughed. "Oh, and this is Joseph Kuntz, Six's handler."

The man held out one hand while he scratched behind Six's ear. "That's right. I'm Six's handler." He grinned. "Liliana and I met in Montana."

Kujo's firm handshake and obvious love for his dog made Liliana like the man even more. "Thank you for coming along on my campaign trail. I never thought I'd need a bomb-sniffing dog to help me run for office, but here you are." She bent toward Six and stopped. "May I pet him?"

Kujo nodded. "Thanks for asking. Not all working dogs are people friendly."

Liliana held out her hand in front of Six. "Hey, big guy. Do you mind if I pet you?"

Six sniffed her hand and stared up into her eyes.

When she reached out to scratch behind his ear, he leaned into her hand.

"Good boy," she said, delighted that he'd taken to her so quickly. "He's beautiful."

"Thank you," Kujo tightened his hand on the dog's lead then reached out and touched Liliana's arm. "Six. Liliana," he said to the dog. Then to Liliana, "Let him sniff your hand again."

She held her hand in front of the dog's nose.

"Liliana," Kujo said in a stern tone.

Six sniffed the hand, then looked up at Kujo.

Kujo nodded. "Good boy."

They took their seats and kept a lively conversation running throughout the meal.

Kujo wasn't a big conversationalist, but he was

happy to talk about how he'd come to adopt Six and when he went to work for Hank Patterson and the Brotherhood Protectors. He was especially proud of his wife, Molly, who worked for the FBI. Mostly, he was head over heels in love with their baby girl, Sarah.

"Don't you miss them when you're on assignment?" Liliana asked.

"More than they'll ever know." Kujo stared down at the photo of his wife holding his daughter.

Liliana's heart contracted. How she'd love to be loved like Kujo loved his family. Sometimes, her journey to help others left her alone in hotel rooms. She'd accepted it as part of the life and career she'd chosen.

Her gaze darted to Dax. She wondered if she'd given up too much, or if she dared to want more, whether it would hurt her career. If she managed to juggle a husband and children, would they resent the time she spent working? Or would she grow to regret missing out on so much of their lives because she was too busy helping others improve their situations?

Most male politicians had stay-at-home spouses who cared for the children and were there full-time to see to their needs.

Liliana didn't know how a life with children would work for her. If she continued to pursue her career as a congresswoman, who would take care of any children that came along? Dax had a job that would take him away from home more than Liliana's. Not that he'd want to marry her.

But if he did, he wouldn't want to be the stay-at-home dad taking care of the children, which meant leaving the children in the care of a stranger.

Again, Dax wasn't signing on to any of her musings. It wasn't the kind of life he'd willingly walk into.

Growing up on the rez with a mother who had worked two jobs to put food on the table, Liliana had spent time with caregivers who, for the most part, had been good. They were members of her tribe who'd stayed home with their own children and earned money caring for others.

It takes a village to raise a child was true in Liliana's case. Her mother had gone to work, knowing someone would make sure Liliana was fed and safe. She hadn't loved Liliana any less.

"Tomorrow will be a busy day," Rachel said. "I'm not sure how Kujo and Six can help out, as we won't have a specific venue for him to inspect beforehand."

"We can walk among the crowd, blending in with others who walk their dogs," Kujo suggested.

Liliana nodded, pulling herself out of her musings about marriage and children in a female politician's life. That she even bothered to mull over far-fetched dreams was a waste of time. It would never happen. Not as long as she was in congress.

If she won the election.

"It will be comforting to know Six is out there, sniffing for explosives," Liliana said. "I admit to a little nervousness getting up in front of people again after the last time."

Rachel reached over the table and covered her hand. "You don't have to do it. Concede the race, and you can go home and not worry that someone is out to get you." She smiled gently. "No one would blame you for wanting out."

If Liliana backed out of the race, she could have any other life she chose to live. Maybe one with a real fiancé and, eventually, children.

Then she thought of all the people counting on her to help make their lives better. "I've come so far," Liliana said. "I've never quit anything in my life."

"Stubborn to a fault if you ask me." Rachel squeezed her hand and smiled. "It makes you who you are. I love you for it. And so do all the people rooting for you."

It was the right thing to do. She just had to get the images of a little Dax and little Liliana out of her mind. They weren't part of her plan, and she'd just have to get over it. "I'm not giving up. I'm in this race to win it."

"That's what I like to hear," Rachel said. "Now, who's up for some dancing? I understand they have a live band in the bar and a dance floor. You two should celebrate your engagement." Rachel's eyes narrowed. "By the way, how did he propose? I'm dying to know. Did he do it right?"

Liliana stared down at her ring. "It was actually on the way here." She glanced up into Dax's eyes. "He found this ring in the Yellowstone visitor's center and popped the question as Ol' Faithful erupted behind us." She smiled. "It was amazing."

Rachel sighed. "He did it right. He must know how much you love Yellowstone and everything about it."

Liliana stared down at the ring on her finger, moisture stinging in her eyes. "And he couldn't have picked a more perfect ring." As perfect as his proposal had been, she couldn't help but feel sad.

A tear slipped down her cheek.

"What's this?" Rachel frowned. "Are you crying?"

Liliana wiped the moisture from her face and forced a smile. "It was so perfect it makes me want to cry happy tears." Why was lying getting easier?

Because the truth made her chest hurt.

Rachel clapped her hands together. "All the more reason to celebrate with a little dancing."

Kujo raised his hand. "We're out. Six isn't so good with loud noises like drums and cymbal crashes. We're going to call it a night."

Rachel laughed. "I'm up for at least one song. I want to see the happy couple make magic on the dance floor, and then I'm going to call it a night as well. I need to catch up on emails and soak in a hot tub."

"I don't know," Liliana said. "I'm pretty tired as well. So much happened today."

Rachel shook her head, pushed back her chair and stood. "No excuses. Besides, dancing can help calm you. Come on. I'll show you where it is. Kujo and Six, sleep well. We'll get an early start at five-thirty. We'll want to be at the breakfast diner by six in the morning. That way, Liliana can catch folks going to work and going home from the night shift."

Liliana stood. Though they'd gone over a lot of subjects on their ride down, they hadn't discussed their views on dancing.

Personally, Liliana loved to dance but hadn't done it since college.

Kujo and Six headed for their room while Rachel led the way to the bar.

Liliana hung back a little and leaned close to Dax. "You don't have to do this. We can go up to the room and call it a night."

He frowned down at her. "I don't mind—unless you don't want to."

She shrugged. "I don't know too many guys who like to dance. You might be one of them. We didn't go over that in our journey of getting to know each other."

He grinned and looped her arm through his. "Don't worry. I'm not one of them. My father would rather die than dance. He refused to perform the first dance with my mother at his own wedding."

"Maybe he was embarrassed because he had no rhythm," Liliana suggested.

His lips pressed together. "All he had to do was hold her and sway, but he wouldn't even do that." He squeezed her arm in his. "Don't worry. I can sway if nothing else." He tipped his head toward Rachel. "We'll give your assistant her celebratory dance and be done."

Butterflies fluttered inside Liliana's belly at the thought of being held in Dax's arms. She knew they were headed in the right direction when she heard strains of music echoing into the hallway.

Rachel hurried to open the bar door and waited as they passed through.

Inside the bar, the lights were turned down low. A three-man band played a fast song in the corner while three couples danced freestyle on the softly lit dance floor.

Rachel found an empty table and waved for a waitress.

After they ordered drinks, Rachel sat back, grinning. "Your engagement might just be the catalyst to push you over the edge in the polls."

Liliana didn't want to talk about the election, marketing or anything else. She was hyper-aware of the man sitting beside her, his thigh touching hers.

A fast song ended, and the band shifted gears into

a slow, sensuous tune.

Heart racing, Liliana braced herself, hoping this was the one Dax would want to dance to. Fast dances were fun but slow...

Hell, slow dancing, if done right, was like making love on the dance floor.

About to ask him herself, Liliana opened her mouth.

Dax held out his hand. "Will you dance with me?"

She smiled, placed her hand in his and let him pull her to her feet and into his arms.

Rachel sighed loudly as they passed her and stepped onto the dance floor.

Dax didn't just sway to the music. He knew how to dance and led her through some dance moves she wasn't familiar with, yet somehow had her following easily. As the song drew to a close, he swung her away from him and then back into his arms, dipping her low.

"Just for show," he whispered.

She looked up into his eyes as he bent over her. God, she prayed he'd kiss her.

Then he did, stealing her breath away in a gentle kiss that melted the bones in her knees.

Around them, the music played on. If it stopped, Liliana couldn't tell. All she could hear was the thundering beat of her heart reverberating against her eardrums and feel the strength of Dax's arms around her.

She wanted the song to go on forever as long as Dax held her in his arms.

CHAPTER 9

WHEN THE SONG FINALLY ENDED, Dax stood with his arm firmly around Liliana's waist, swaying to the beat. "See," he said, "I can sway."

She laughed, leaned back and smiled up into his eyes. "That was amazing. Where did you learn to dance like that?"

He grinned. "From a woman I met at McP's bar in San Diego. She happened to teach ballroom dancing. I was so inept that she took pity on me and gave me lessons for half price. At first, I saw no point. Then she took me to a local dance hall. Because I could lead decently by then, all the women wanted to dance with me." His grin widened. "I don't think I sat once that night. Like everything I set out to do, I gave it my all, learning as much as I could until I deployed. That was my last deployment with the Navy. I never made it back to McP's or to that dance instructor."

"Were you in love with her?" Liliana asked before she could think better of it.

He laughed. "I loved her like an older sister. She must've been in her fifties. Because she danced so much, she didn't look her age. She liked to hang out at McP's to talk with the bartender, who happened to be an old gunnery sergeant from the Marines. I think he had a thing for her." Dax tipped his head to one side. "Sandy was a great gal. I need to look her up and see where she is now."

The band started another song, this one with a Latin beat. Dax led her in a salsa, making it seem easy as well when it was all Dax's doing.

When the song ended, Liliana was flush with exertion and smiling. She'd never had so much fun dancing. "It's too bad your father didn't meet your dance instructor before his wedding to your mother."

"He wouldn't have taken any lessons from anyone. My old man swore he'd never wanted to dance and never would. Now he couldn't dance, even if he wanted." Dax shook his head. "He didn't know what he was missing." He stared down into her eyes. "I'm glad I learned. I love the way you fit in my arms and the way you move with me, not against me. Dancing is a partnership."

Liliana could listen to him talk about dancing all night long, but the band had stopped playing, and its members were packing up their instruments.

Rachel met them on the dance floor. "You two

were amazing." She wrapped her arms around both of them and brought them in for a bear hug. Then she let go and stepped away. "I got some great shots for your social media. I'll post them tonight, then I'm going to bed. See ya in the morning, bright and early."

"We're headed that way, too," Liliana said. "In a few minutes." She wanted Rachel to get a good head start before they followed, giving Liliana more alone time with Dax in a more neutral environment. Back in the room was like sitting on a powder keg with a short fuse.

"Want to have a drink?" Dax asked.

Liliana let go of the breath she hadn't realized she'd been holding. "Yes. I'd love that."

They returned to their table. After the waitress took their order, Liliana looked everywhere but at Dax, trying to come up with some interesting conversation and failing miserably.

The waitress delivered their drinks, and still, Liliana couldn't come up with anything interesting. "What do you think of Wyoming so far?" she asked.

"This side of the state is amazing.

Liliana laughed. "The eastern side of the state is flat and arid, full of big farms and ranches with little water and bitterly cold winters."

"I can imagine how brutal the winds are with little to slow them down," Dax sipped his beer and glanced around the room as if noting every entry and exit point.

Liliana glanced around at the people sitting quietly, talking over a glass of wine or whiskey. Not one of them looked like someone who was keeping tabs on her with the intention of eliminating her as a candidate. "Do you think the person who targeted me could be in this room watching me?"

"The thought crossed my mind. Jason had an accomplice who has yet to be identified. For that matter, they both could've been hired by someone else calling the shots."

Liliana's eyes narrowed as she glanced around the room again, studying each guest carefully. "That someone would have the money to pay guys and keep his own hands clean of the dirty work."

"Right," Dax said. "Someone with something to lose if you get that seat in congress. What programs or initiatives are you proposing to shut down?"

Liliana frowned as she thought back through her campaign promises and some of the litigation she'd been involved with protecting her state from big business taking advantage of loopholes.

"I promised to enforce the clean-up of old mines and to stop land development encroachment on national park and reservation lands. Water rights can be tricky and important to downstream locations dependent on them."

"Do you recall any big businesses in particular

that might benefit from one of the other candidates winning instead of you?" Dax asked.

"Ten Mule Mining Corporation has been fighting with the Wyoming supreme court and the EPA over funding the restoration of one of their open pit mines," Liliana said. "I was on the litigation team to enforce the restoration."

"Do you know the owner of that mine?"

"It's a corporation with a board of directors."

"What about the CEO?"

"Robert Davis. They pay him huge bonuses for keeping expenses down." Liliana frowned. "You think he might be so motivated by the money that he would kill me to keep me from passing legislation that would impact the mining company?"

"The C-4 explosives came from a mining operation near Gillette. Is the Ten Mule Mining Corporation near Gillette?"

She nodded, still frowning. "It is, but that would be too obvious, don't you think?"

Dax shrugged. "Davis could've gotten sloppy or paid someone else to take the fall by making it look like a robbery."

"Maybe."

"What about the land developer?" Dax asked.

"THEnterprises is the company I mentioned to Stone and Swede—the one pushing to build a mega-resort bordering Yellowstone National Park and the Wind River Reservation."

"Have you had any run-ins with their owner or CEO?"

"I've met Tate Harris in court. He's a high-powered, big-money guy who's used to getting his way. He didn't like that I put his project on hold until the full scale of it could be reviewed. He liked it even less when the state of Wyoming put the kibosh on the proposal for roads cutting through the park and the rez."

"I'll put in a call to Swede to see if THEnterprises or Tate Harris have contributed to the other candidates. I'll also have him check and see if he can find anything on the mining company where they got the C4 as well as the Ten Mule Mining Company."

"Could it just be Jason Monahan out for revenge? He could've gotten a friend or hired someone to steal the C-4."

Dax nodded. "True. The fact that he's not talking makes me think he might be protecting someone else."

"And he doesn't want to say anything that will put him back in jail," Liliana said. "Although, the evidence found in his trailer is enough to put him back behind bars all by itself."

Dax finished his beer and set the mug on the table. "We should call it a night. You have a busy day tomorrow campaigning and a speech to give tomorrow night at the fundraiser."

Liliana's heart skipped several beats and raced

ahead to the thought of sleeping in the same suite as the handsome man sitting across from her.

He stood and held her chair as she rose.

Her shoulder brushed against his, sending electric shocks through her body. She took a quick step away, catching her toe on the chair leg. Liliana stumbled.

Dax caught her around the waist and pulled her against him to steady her. "Careful," he whispered against her ear.

Her hands rested against his chest, her pulse pounding so hard she was sure he could hear it. "Thank you."

He didn't let go of her immediately but held her so gently she could move anytime she wanted.

The problem was she didn't want to move. She liked how warm and strong his arms were around her and didn't want him to let go.

Ever.

The thought shocked her almost as much as the electric current his touch generated inside her body.

Liliana stepped back. "We should go to bed." Her eyes widened when she realized what she'd said. "I mean, we should go to the suite and sleep. Not that we should go to bed together. That's not what I meant at all. After all, you're only there to protect me, not to sleep with me. I wouldn't want you to feel like you had to do anything. We're just together for the campaign, nothing more, right? Then you'll go your way, and I'll go mine, and we'll never see each other again. Will we?"

He touched a finger to her lips and chuckled. "Do I make you nervous, Miss Lightfeather?"

Her cheeks on fire, Liliana closed her eyes and resisted the temptation to kiss the finger touching her lips.

When he removed it, she opened her eyes. "I'm sorry. I don't know what's wrong with me."

"It's been a long day," he said and pulled her arm through the crook of his elbow. "You need rest."

"That's right. That must be it." She walked along-side him to the elevator and stepped inside. The mirrors reflected a man—a very handsome one—only doing his duty and a woman who could pretend she was all right but, deep down, was on the verge of insanity.

She wanted to throw caution to the wind and take Dax to bed with her.

When the elevator door opened on the top floor, Liliana stepped out, concentrating on the mantra going through her head.

He's the protector. You're the client. Hands off.

She took her room key card out of her clutch and ran it through the door scanner. The door opened.

"Me first," Dax said. "Wait here." He made a quick check and returned. "All clear."

Liliana crossed the threshold. As soon as she did, she stepped in front of him. "Thank you for a lovely evening and the dancing." She had all good intentions of leaving it at that and going alone to her bedroom.

Then she did a bad thing. She leaned up on her toes and brushed her lips across his. It wasn't enough. She slipped her hand around the back of his neck and pulled him closer, deepening the kiss.

Dax kicked the door closed behind her and pulled Liliana into his arms. "I promised myself I wouldn't do this," he said. "But woman, I can't resist."

Her breath caught at the fire in his eyes. "Some promises were meant to be broken," she whispered, pulling him down.

He crushed her mouth with his, his tongue pushing past her teeth to tangle with hers.

Liliana couldn't have stopped if she'd tried. And she wasn't trying to stop at all. In fact, she couldn't get close enough. As if on its own, her leg slid behind his and curled around his calf. The deeper the kiss, the higher her leg climbed, pressing her sex against his thigh.

Not enough.

She wanted him.

All of him.

Inside her.

Now.

As if he heard her thoughts, Dax's hands slipped downward, over the swell of her buttocks to cup the backs of her thighs. Then he lifted her.

She wrapped her legs around his waist and her

arms around his neck as he carried her into the bedroom.

Once there, he let her slide down his body, his hands sliding up under the hem of her dress.

She reached behind her to unzip the garment, only to have him brush her hands away.

"Let me." Dax turned her around and pressed his lips to the back of her neck. Then he pulled the tab on the back of her dress, lowering the zipper to the small of her back.

Liliana shivered in anticipation, her body on fire.

Dax slid the straps of her dress over her shoulders, ever so slowly, pressing his lips to the exposed skin first on one side, then the other.

Her breath catching in her throat, Liliana could barely stand to wait for another second to get naked and then strip him of his clothes.

Once the straps rounded the curve of her shoulders, the dress slipped down her body, pooling at her high-heeled feet. She hadn't worn a bra with the dress because of the tiny straps. All she wore were heels and her lacy bikini panties.

Dax wrapped his hands around her naked waist and pulled her against him. "Tell me to stop...and I will." He moved her hair aside and kissed the back of her neck, his hands coming up to cup her breasts.

"Don't stop...please." Her words came out as a whisper, her breathing alternating between being caught in her lungs and whooshing out with his every touch.

He bent, scooped her up in his arms and deposited her on the bed, leaning over to kiss her again.

Then he straightened, shucked his shoes and clothes and climbed up on the bed beside her.

She laughed. "I feel a bit overdressed."

He drew his finger along the side of her cheek. "I kind of like the heels. I'll take care of the rest."

The finger slid over her jaw and down the length of her throat, eventually stopping at the swell of her breast. He tweaked the nipple between his thumb and forefinger until it beaded into a tight point.

Liliana writhed beneath him. Eager for more, she guided his hand to the other breast, where he toyed with it until he had her moaning. Then he took the breast in his mouth, tongued, nipped and flicked it.

Abandoning her breasts, he moved down her torso, blazing a path of kisses and nips until he reached the black lace panties she'd worn beneath her dress. Hooking his thumb in the elastic band, he dragged them over her hips and down her legs. On his way back up, he spread her thighs, moved in and parted her folds.

The first flick of his tongue on her clit sent a shockwave of sensations throughout her body. The next flick had her arching her back off the bed, urging him to take more.

He did, laving, flicking and sucking at that most sensitive place until Liliana shot over the edge, her body pulsing with her release all the way to the end.

When at last she sank back against the mattress, she dug her hands into his hair and tugged gently. "I want you."

He leaned over the side of the bed, snagged his trousers and fished his wallet out of the back pocket. For a few tense moments, he sorted through it, finally coming up with a foil packet.

She took it from him, tore it open and rolled it over his engorged staff. Then she guided him to her entrance.

He leaned over her and claimed her mouth in a long, sexy kiss. At the same time, he slid into her slick entrance, moving slowly.

Impatient to have all of him filling her, she gripped his hips and brought him all the way home.

Dax groaned and remained buried long enough for her to adjust to his length and girth. Then he pulled out and pushed back in, increasing his speed until he rocked in and out of her in sharp, deep strokes.

Liliana rose to meet him, lifting her hips off the mattress, her hands still on his ass. Everything about him felt good and right. Tension mounted inside until she came apart in a second release.

At the same time, Dax thrust deep and held steady, his cock throbbing against her channel.

Dax dropped down onto her and rolled her over into his arms, maintaining their intimate connection. He kissed her forehead, her eyelids, the tip of her nose and, finally, her mouth, lingering there to nibble her bottom lip.

"You're an amazing woman, Liliana Lightfeather."

"And you're...you're...wow." She laughed and captured his face between her palms. "I'm at a loss for words. That was beyond incredible. Can we do it again?"

Dax chuckled. "Give me a minute."

"Take all the time you need," she said. "We have all night."

"You're insatiable," he said, slipping a strand of her hair behind her ear.

"If I am, it's because you inspire me." Liliana captured his hand in hers and pressed it to her cheek. Pretending to be in love was getting too easy. If she wasn't careful, she could fall in love with her protector.

She might already be halfway there.

For a moment, she wished they could stay in this bed, in this suite, to hide away from the rest of the world and just make love.

Too bad, the morning would come. They'd have to face reality, a campaign, a killer and, eventually, move on with their lives.

Alone.

CHAPTER 10

FOR STAYING up into the early hours of the morning, Dax still felt refreshed, rejuvenated and ready to face the world.

Making love with Liliana might have been a mistake, but he couldn't regret it. Not for a single minute. She was fun, sexy and so passionate, he'd had a hard time keeping up with her. Still, he'd given it his all, finally falling into a deep sleep a couple hours before the alarm went off.

They showered together and dressed for the day, stopping to kiss, snuggle and hold each other between putting on jeans, shirts and shoes.

When they finally made it down to the lobby, Rachel was waiting with Kujo and Six.

"Oh, good," Rachel said. "I was about to come get you. We'll have to hustle to get to the diner by six."

"I'm ready," Liliana said, a smile lifting the corners

of her lips. She hadn't stopped smiling since the alarm clock had gone off.

Rachel gave her a pointed stare. "You're super happy this morning. What's got into you?"

Liliana's cheeks flushed a bright pink. "Nothing. It's a beautiful morning in Wyoming. Can't a girl just be happy?"

Rachel looked from Liliana to Dax and back to Liliana. "It's him, right? I don't think I've seen you this happy. Ever. He must be treating you right." She winked at Dax. "Whatever you're doing, don't stop."

Dax caught the shadow fleetingly crossing Liliana's face before it disappeared behind her practiced smile. He hated that her happiness dimmed at Rachel's words. He hated that, all too soon, he'd have to stop doing what he was doing to make Liliana happy. It was all a farce with some temporary, mutually agreed-upon benefits.

Her earlier good mood had done something to Dax. He found himself glad that he was partially responsible for her happiness. If things were different... If Liliana wasn't going into politics and eventually moving to D.C.... If he was someone more in league with the pretty candidate, he might consider breaking his promise never to marry.

Liliana needed a man of her caliber. Someone who could mix and mingle with powerful people— not a combat veteran more comfortable in a worn pair of jeans than a suit and tie.

Some of the joy of the day faded at the thought of Liliana marrying a stiff-suited attorney or politician. Someone she could show off in the big city.

Dax had no desire to live in or around D.C. Too much traffic and hot air. If he were the right man for Liliana, he'd do it. She deserved someone who would have her back in the dog-eat-dog arena of government.

With Liliana on his arm, he stepped out of the resort lobby into the cool, mountain air and drew in a deep breath.

The more time he spent in Montana and Wyoming, the more he loved its wide-open spaces, crisp, clean air and Liliana.

He glanced down at her jet-black hair, smoothed back in a loose ponytail at the back of her head. With her high cheekbones and brown-black eyes, she was stunning.

He wanted to take her back up to their suite, rip off her jeans and crisp, white blouse and make love to her all over again.

She chose that moment to look up at him and smile.

His heart squeezed hard in his chest.

"What are you thinking?" she asked.

"You don't want to know," he said softly.

Liliana chuckled and leaned into him. "It's probably the same thing I'm thinking. If I wasn't committed to a day of campaigning, we would."

He grinned. "What you're saying is that I won't convince you to play hooky and go back to the room for the rest of the morning."

She looked up at him, her eyes flaring. "You're tempting me."

"Stop it, you two," Rachel called out. "You need to focus on winning votes, not whatever you did behind closed doors." She held up her hand. "Don't tell me. I don't want to know. It would only make me even more envious."

"I had the valet bring our vehicles around." Rachel stopped next to a dark gray sedan. "This is my ride. We'll take separate vehicles so that I can get back early enough to make sure everything is ready for tonight's fundraiser."

Kujo stepped forward. "I'd offer you both a ride in my truck but, as well-behaved as Six is, he sheds. You won't want to be covered in dog hair when you're meeting the public." Kujo walked Six around all three vehicles, circled back to his truck and loaded Six into the back seat.

Liliana and Dax continued past Rachel and Kujo's vehicles to Dax's truck.

He opened the passenger door for Liliana and helped her up into her seat. "If I haven't already told you, you look just as beautiful in your jeans and boots as you did in your dress last night."

She leaned down and kissed him. "Thank you."

"It's a smart choice when meeting the working

folks. It's one thing to look professional, but it helps that you can look approachable as well."

She smiled. "That was the plan."

"And you look natural. Not like a city girl playing dress-up in western clothes."

Her lips twisted in a wry grin. "I grew up in jeans and boots, and I can ride bareback or in a saddle. We were all over the reservation on horseback."

Another reason to love this woman. She was badass.

Love.

As Dax rounded the front of the truck to the other side, he pressed a hand to his chest to ease the knot forming there.

So many years ago, he'd sworn off commitment and marriage. In the short time he'd known Liliana, she'd blown a hole right through his promise to himself. He'd thought more about a lifetime with one person in the past twenty-four hours than he'd ever done before. Not just any person. Only one.

Liliana.

He slid into the seat beside her and started the engine. "Ready for a day of smiling and kissing babies?" he asked.

She nodded. "Bring on the babies. They'll be voters someday, too."

He followed Kujo and Rachel into town and parked outside the diner that was the locals' favorite.

"We can get something to eat while we're here,"

she said. "The food must be good, based on the number of cars in the parking lot."

Dax studied the vehicles and the people entering and leaving the diner. "Did you advertise this meet-and-greet to anyone?"

Liliana shook her head. "I didn't want this to be a big deal. I wanted to meet the real locals, not the outsiders who'd want to gawk at the congressional candidate."

He felt a little better, knowing this wasn't a staged event. If Jason wasn't the only one out to get Liliana, that person wouldn't have known she'd be at the diner this morning. He wouldn't have had time to set charges or a surprise attack.

Nonetheless, Dax was glad to see Kujo and Six walking around the outside of the diner.

Rachel joined them at the door. "Ready?"

Liliana squared her shoulders, lifted her chin and smiled. "I'm ready."

For the next two hours, Liliana shook hands, smiled and greeted every patron of the diner, the staff, owner and cooks. She sat with customers while they drank coffee and talked about things that concerned them.

They left smiling, thanking her for listening.

She made them promise to vote, even if it wasn't for her.

When the steady stream of customers slowed to a trickle, Rachel herded them out the door and onto

Main Street where Liliana went door to door, meeting business owners and their customers.

Throughout the morning, Liliana smiled, attentive and gracious.

Dax's chest swelled with pride at how good she was with people and how genuine her concern was for their wellbeing.

"There's a parade this afternoon for the start of their county fair," Rachel said. "I arranged for a local to drive you in the parade in a rented convertible with banners affixed to either side."

"You're amazing, Rachel," Liliana said. "I don't know how you fit all you do into a day. You should be the one running for congress."

"No thank you. I like being ground support for your launch. I don't have to stand in front of people and talk all day. Besides, I like planning and organizing. It's my superpower."

"It definitely is a superpower." Liliana hugged Rachel. "I'm glad you decided to come to work with me."

"Me, too. It's been a challenge I've enjoyed." Rachel dug in her purse and pulled out a powder compact, a tube of lipstick and a brush. "Here. Freshen up. Your car should be arriving right about..." she glanced up, "now. There he is. Good. And the banners are perfect. The voters will see your name in bold colors and remember it when they go to the polls."

"Should I walk alongside the car?" Dax asked.

Rachel shook her head. "No way. Ride with Liliana. The public will want to see her fiancé. I've already posted to social media about the two of you and the fact you're a combat veteran and Navy SEAL. There's been so much more interaction since that post that I think they'll be looking for you."

Dax nodded, glad he'd be in the vehicle with her. If anything happened, he'd be right there.

As it was, the parade went off without a hitch, until the last block before the floats dispersed.

Liliana had smiled and waved the entire time with Dax waving beside her.

Dax could see the end in sight at the next block. People were climbing down from floats, laughing and smiling.

As the convertible in which Dax and Liliana had been riding slowed, a delivery truck shot out of a side street, headed straight for the convertible.

Dax didn't have time to warn the driver. He flung himself over the back of the seat, grabbed the steering wheel and pulled it hard to the left.

Instead of T-boning the convertible, the delivery truck clipped the front end and spun them around. Still draped over the back of the driver's seat, Dax was thrown into the front passenger seat and slid onto the floorboard.

He pushed up in time to see the delivery truck ram into the side of a building.

Dax turned to where Liliana had been sitting on the back end of the car with her feet in the seat. She wasn't there.

"Liliana!" he yelled.

"I'm okay," her muffled voice came from the back seat.

Dax leaned over the back of the passenger seat to find Liliana on her back on the floorboard, looking up.

"Are you all right?" Dax reached down, grabbed her hand and helped her to sit in the back seat.

Liliana nodded. "I was lucky the impact knocked me forward into the car and not out onto the pavement." She glanced around at the people darting around. "Was anyone hurt?"

The driver was unharmed, and there had been enough distance between their vehicle and the floats before and after them that no one on the floats was hurt.

"Do me a favor and stay down," Dax said. "I want to check out the truck and see if the driver is still in it."

After Liliana sank low in her seat, Dax hopped out of the convertible and ran toward the truck, circling around behind it to come up on the passenger side. He climbed up on the step, yanked open the door and stared into the empty cab.

At first, he thought the driver had escaped. Then he noticed a block had been affixed to the gas pedal.

The truck ramming into their convertible had not been an accident. Someone had rigged the accelerator and jumped out before the truck took off, heading straight for their car.

Dax hurried back to the convertible, afraid the attacker might make another move while Liliana was a sitting duck in the car.

"Is the driver okay?" Liliana asked.

Dax shook his head. "There wasn't one. Someone rigged the truck to ram into us. Whoever did is probably long gone."

He called 911 and reported the incident. Liliana called Rachel who'd gone back to the resort to make sure the stage, mics and sound system were working correctly for Liliana's speech that night.

"Oh, sweet Jesus," Rachel exclaimed after hearing about the accident. "Can you get to your truck?"

"Yes," Liliana replied.

"I'll let Kujo know to meet you at your truck to check it before you get in."

Liliana relayed Rachel's message to Dax.

They had to wait around until the police came to investigate and collect latent prints. They left as the tow truck arrived to take the delivery truck to an impound lot where it would be further investigated.

Liliana and Dax walked the few blocks back to where they'd parked his truck and met the driver of the convertible at the beginning of the parade.

Kujo stood with Six near the tailgate. "Glad to see you two made it. Rachel told me what happened."

Dax nodded toward his truck. "Anything?"

Kujo shook his head. "Six didn't find anything. As far as we can tell, your truck is safe."

Dax pulled Liliana into the circle of his arms. "Good. We're headed back to the resort."

"We'll take the lead," Kujo said.

Dax helped Liliana up into the truck and closed the door.

The drive back to the resort was blessedly uneventful. When they arrived, the manager was quick to appear.

"We heard what happened," the manager said. "We're so sorry the incident occurred in our little town. It's usually a quiet, safe place. Is there anything we can do to help?"

"No," Liliana said. "I just want to get into the hot tub for a while before the event this evening."

The manager stood beside the truck, wringing his hands. "In light of the attack today, do we need to cancel the fundraiser?"

Liliana shook her head. "No. We should be okay. No one can drive a truck up into the banquet hall. Not easily, anyway."

Dax wasn't sure the fundraiser was a good idea. Not with someone still making Liliana a target.

If he had his way, Dax would take Liliana into the mountains and hide her away until after the election.

Someone really didn't want Liliana to make it to election day, and he'd come close to succeeding.

Dax wasn't certain he would be enough to protect Liliana. When he had a spare minute alone, he'd call Stone and get his opinion. Since spiriting the woman off into the mountains wasn't an option, he might need help keeping her safe. The attacker was using whatever means were available and didn't care if anyone else got in the way.

CHAPTER 11

BACK IN THEIR SUITE, Liliana paced the length of the sitting room, her boots clicking against the shiny tile.

Dax, Rachel, Kujo and Six had gathered in the suite after they'd arrived.

"Someone could've been hurt or killed today." She paused and met Rachel's gaze. "Someone besides me. I need to call off the town visits and go back to the reservation."

"You can't do that. You're too close to election day," Rachel said.

"I can't keep putting others at risk." She looked to Dax. "You could've been killed."

"I'm too damned stubborn to get killed." He crossed the floor and took her hands in his. "I'm not backing down, and I don't think you should either."

"We have a couple of hours until the fundraiser,"

Rachel said. "Why don't you make use of the hot tub and relax. I'll have some food sent up."

"I don't feel good about this fundraiser," Liliana confessed.

"I'll call Stone and see if he can spare a couple more guys to post around the ballroom or exterior perimeter."

"I'll spend the next couple of hours with Six going through the ballroom where the dinner will be held."

"He didn't use explosives in the last attack, who's to say he'll use them again?" Liliana scrubbed a hand over her face. "He used a truck as a lethal weapon."

"The ballroom isn't on the ground level," Rachel pointed out. "He can't drive a truck into that portion of the building."

Liliana drew in a breath and let it out, reminding herself to breathe. "I just don't want anyone else to get hurt."

"I'll get the resort manager to call in his entire security staff if we have to," Rachel said. "We need this fundraiser, and we need the people to vote for you."

"Yeah, but is it worth losing people?" Liliana looked from Dax to Rachel and back. "You could've been thrown from that convertible and sustained life-threatening injuries."

"I'm fine," Dax said. "No one was hurt. If you need this fundraiser, we can make it happen."

She chewed on her bottom lip for several more

moments before she sighed. "Okay. We'll do the fundraiser, but I want to look at all other events before we decide we'll do them. Until this attacker is caught, none of us are safe."

Rachel, Kujo and Six left the suite.

Dax opened his arms, and Liliana fell into them.

"I was so scared," she said. "When I fell onto the floorboard, I couldn't see you."

He smoothed her hair back from her forehead. Her ponytail had been lost in the commotion, allowing her long, straight locks to fall forward into her face. The locks were soft and silky between his fingers.

"Get your swimsuit on. We'll soak in the hot tub. It'll help calm you."

He walked with her into the bedroom and waited while she dug through her clothes until she found her suit.

"What about you?" she asked. "Did you bring a suit?"

He shook his head. "No, but I have gym shorts I can use."

Once she had her suit in hand, he turned her toward the bathroom. "Go change. I'll be ready when you come back out." Though he wanted to, he didn't offer to change with her or to make love to her while they did.

Liliana entered the bathroom.

Dax closed the door between them.

He hurriedly changed into his shorts and called Stone.

He brought him up to speed on what had happened at the parade and asked, "Can you spare anyone to come down for this fundraiser?"

"It's too far to drive, and a storm system is moving in from the southwest. It'll hit you before it hits us. I doubt Hank's plane could bring us down before the event. I'm sorry, man. You have Kujo and Six. I'll put someone on the road, but they won't be there until after the event begins."

"I'm okay with that. Better late to the party than not at all," Dax said. "Thanks, man. I knew I could count on you."

"I hope you have an uneventful evening. Expect one or more of the gang to arrive sometime during the evening. And keep your head down.

"Yes, sir." As Dax ended the call, the bathroom door opened, and Liliana stepped out wearing a one-piece, forest green swimsuit with a plunging neckline. She'd pulled her hair up high on her head and secured it with a clip.

He took her hand and led her out onto the balcony where the hot tub stood.

They climbed in, and he turned on the jets and settled back in the water, thankful they were on the top floor, out of range of snipers or people dropping things on them from above.

Liliana scooted close to him and reached for his

hand beneath the water.

He brought her hand up to his lips and pressed a kiss to it. "Everything will be all right."

"I hope you're right," she said.

They stayed in the tub for thirty minutes. By the time they got out, Liliana seemed more relaxed. She showered and changed into the outfit she had selected for the fundraiser. The floor-length sheath in shimmering silver complimented her dark beauty to perfection.

Dax wore the same black suit he'd worn the night before with a black shirt and gray tie.

He held out his arm. "You look amazing."

"Is this dress too flashy? I don't want them to think I'm only concerned about fancy clothes and not the issues."

"It's perfect. You look confident and intelligent. When you speak, your passion for your work will outshine even this dress." He smiled.

She frowned. "It is too flashy."

When she turned back to the bedroom, he stopped her with a hand on her arm. "It's not too flashy. If anything, it says you're not afraid of anything."

"But I am afraid—afraid that by continuing this campaign, others will become collateral damage." She took his hand in hers. "I don't want that to happen to anyone." Her voice lowered, and she stared into his eyes. "Especially you."

His chest tightened at the concern she had for him. His own family had never looked at him that way. His father didn't seem to give two shits about him. His mother had abandoned him.

Standing before him was a woman he'd known for such a short time, willing to give up her dream of becoming a representative of her state to keep him from being hurt.

"Sweetheart, I'm willing to take the risk. You're a good person. The people of this state need someone like you to represent them. Don't deprive them of the opportunity to make that decision."

She stood for a long moment as if weighing the pros and cons. Finally, she nodded. "I'm not a quitter. Let's get this fundraiser over with. I have work to do."

He grinned. "That's the woman we know and love. Let's go get 'em."

Dax was proud to escort Liliana Lightfeather to the ballroom where the dinner was held. He was also glad to see that the resort had beefed up the security staff.

They'd funneled the guests through one door, checking each against an attendees' roster before they were allowed to enter. The other doors had been locked from the inside. Two security guards stood at the entrance to the ballroom to keep any unauthorized persons from entering.

Once inside, Dax and Liliana were escorted to a

table at the front of the room, closest to the stage.

Rachel and Kujo stood beside the table with Six lying on the floor at Kujo's feet.

Five other name cards were located at their table.

"You've been seated with the guests who've contributed the most to your campaign," Rachel said.

"I take it you've done your homework and can give me a quick profile on each?" Liliana cocked an eyebrow.

"You betcha." Rachel grinned. "Mr. and Mrs. Alan Buttram of Buttram Technologies. They own several manufacturing facilities in the state, which produce electronic components for the Department of Defense. They're very patriotic and believe in keeping industry in the US."

"I've heard of them," Liliana said. "Their corporations hire locally when they can and even provide training to get the skills they need."

Rachel nodded. "Colin and Connor Satterwhite are brothers, who've built a multi-million-dollar corporation from an idea and a shoe-string budget in their parent's garage. They're one of the fastest growing companies in the state."

"And they're in their mid-thirties, so young to have come this far," Liliana commented.

Rachel nodded toward a man with salt-and-pepper gray hair, wearing a gray, pinstripe suit coming through the door. "Our last guest at the table might be of interest to you. Tate Harris."

Dax tensed. "Tate Harris of THEnterprises?"

Rachel nodded. "He's contributed more to Liliana's campaign than the Buttrams and the Satterwhites together."

Liliana frowned. "Why didn't I know this?"

"I didn't know it until I got the most current list of attendees and their contribution amounts," Rachel said. "He is the most recent contributor, having deposited the funds yesterday."

"Does he think he can buy my cooperation and support of his land development?" Liliana shook her head slightly, her gaze following the man moving between the tables toward them.

Dax stiffened as the man stopped in front of Liliana. He stood ready in case Harris tried anything to hurt Liliana. He didn't like how close the man stood to her. If he was armed, he could easily take her down.

Harris held out a hand to Liliana. "Miss Lightfeather, I'm Tate Harris of THEnterprises. It's a pleasure to meet you and to be a part of your campaign to win the Wyoming seat in congress."

Liliana took the man's hand and even gave him a tight smile. "Mr. Harris. It's nice to meet you. Thank you for your support and contribution."

He turned toward Dax. "I understand you're to be congratulated on your recent engagement." He held out his hand. "It's an honor to meet a combat veteran and Navy SEAL."

Dax took his hand and gave it a firm shake, staring straight into the man's dull gray eyes. "Mr. Harris."

Harris's hand was cool, but firm, his expression poker straight, unreadable.

Dax didn't trust the man.

The Buttrams arrived. Rachel introduced them to Liliana and the others at the table. Right behind them were Colin and Connor Satterwhite, who weren't much older than Liliana and Dax.

They took their seats, the Satterwhite brothers diving into a conversation about the state of Wyoming and ways they could attract more industry, and thus, employment opportunities. They exuded a level of energy and passion that kept the discussion going throughout the meal.

Thankfully, Rachel had arranged the name tags, placing Harris between the Satterwhites and Kujo, with Six at his feet, on the other side of the table from Liliana. Dax listened attentively, while keeping a close watch on everything around them but mostly on Tate Harris.

The Buttrams and Satterwhites spoke about the future of manufacturing in the state. Harris sat back and listened for a while. After the main course had been cleared and dessert was served, Harris lifted his coffee mug and paused. "Attracting industry is one way to bring more jobs to Wyoming, but this state's economy is tied to mining, tourism and agriculture. Manufacturing is less than 6% of the state output."

"A fact we hope to change," Colin Satterwhite said.

The Buttrams nodded.

"Wyoming is also the least populated state in the union," Harris continued. "If you bring in more manufacturing jobs, who will fill those positions? We already have a shortage of employees to fill the open jobs."

"Mr. Harris, you're in land development, are you not?" Connor Satterwhite asked.

Harris nodded. "I build resorts, which cater to tourism, the second largest contributor to the state's economy. Tourism employs over twelve percent of the state's workforce, even more than the number one contributor to the economy, mining, at just over 3 % and the almost 3.5% employed by manufacturing."

"And your point is?" Alan Buttram asked.

Out of the corner of his eye, Dax could see Liliana's lips twitch. She probably wanted to ask the same question but hadn't wanted to poke a sore spot with the man. Namely, the stalling of the man's projected mega-resorts.

"Tourism brings more jobs, employs more people and provides the most income to the state of Wyoming," Harris said. "Projects to increase the number of tourists who visit our state will increase the number of jobs and money generated for our economy."

Liliana leaned forward. "People come to Wyoming because of several key natural attractions. There has to be a balance between increasing our GNP and protecting our natural resources. It's our duty as residents of the state to be good stewards of the land that has been set aside as National Parks, National Forests and National Monuments. We have to protect them in order for them to still be around for future generations to enjoy and appreciate." She met and held Harris's stare.

A man stepped up onto the stage, tapped the microphone and announced, "Ladies and gentlemen, please welcome Miss Liliana Lightfeather, independent candidate for the US Congress to represent the people and the state of Wyoming."

Rachel leaned into Liliana's shoulder. "It's time."

Liliana gave a tight smile to the guests at the table. "If you'll excuse me, I'm the keynote speaker. We can continue this discussion afterward."

Harris's eyes narrowed. "Yes, we will."

Dax rose and held Liliana's chair as she stood. When she started to step away, he reached for her hand and held her in place. "Want me to go with you?" he whispered.

She looked up into his eyes, her smile more genuine. "Thank you, but no. I have to do this on my own."

"You've got this." He bent to brush his lips across hers, releasing her hand at the same time.

Dax continued to stand as Liliana walked up to the stage and took the mic from the MC.

Once she was on stage, Dax took his seat and listened as Liliana spoke of a little girl raised on the Wind River Indian Reservation, who hadn't had a penny to her name but had worked hard to do more for her family, her people, and eventually, the people of her state.

Her sincere desire to help others came across in her tone, her demeanor and her confidence that she would make a difference, representing the people. She promised to do her best to protect their livelihoods at the same time as she fought to protect the natural resources that made the state so unique and beautiful. She promised to listen to people of all races and economic statuses.

Dax was mesmerized by her physical beauty as well as the beauty of her conviction. As he glanced around the room, he noticed that every gaze was on Liliana, each individual caught up in her passion and pride for the state where she'd been born and raised. Their state.

As she concluded her speech with a heartfelt thank you to those who contributed to her campaign, she added a request for everyone to get out and vote, whether it was for her or for another candidate. "Your vote is your voice. Let it be heard."

The room erupted in applause and a standing ovation.

Dax looked across the table at Harris.

The man pushed to his feet without clapping like everyone else in the room.

Liliana smiled and thanked the audience, then handed the MC the microphone.

"There will be a social in the bar for those who would like to speak with Miss Lightfeather in person."

As Liliana turned to walk away, a loud bang pierced the silence, and smoke billowed up from beneath the stage.

Pandemonium erupted. Women screamed, and everyone rushed for the exits.

Dax glanced up. Why hadn't the fire suppression system kicked in?

Kujo yelled, "Get Liliana. I'll get the others out."

Dax was already racing for the stage and Liliana.

Flames leaped up the fabric skirting along the front of the raised platform and climbed the curtains on either side.

The closer he came to the stage, the more the smoke burned his eyes and blurred his view of Liliana.

Through the flames and smoke, he thought he saw her turn toward the back of the stage with the MC. Though the smoke was thick, Dax was almost certain a door opened, and they ducked through it.

The flames burned hot, consuming the fabric curtains. They fell onto the stage, making it impossible for Dax to follow Liliana.

He looked back at the crush of people pushing against the exit doors.

Shouts went up.

"The doors are blocked!"

"We can't get out!"

"We're trapped!"

With no other option, Dax dashed back to the table, yanked the tablecloth out from under the plates and glasses, soaking it with their leftover drinks. He wrapped the damp tablecloth around his head, shoulders and face and ran up onto the stage, diving through the flames and smoke.

He couldn't see Liliana or the MC. They had to have made it out the back door of the stage.

Bending low, he stumbled through the haze, his eyes and lungs burning. He didn't stop until he reached the back wall. He felt along the wall until he found the door, fumbled for the handle and tried to turn it.

It was locked.

With flames at his back and smoke all around him, he couldn't go back the way he'd come. He had to get through the door.

Dax cocked his leg and kicked as hard as he could. The door didn't open, but the sound of splitting wood encouraged him to try again.

With heat bearing down on him and smoke beginning to burn his lungs and eyes, he kicked again and again, putting everything he had into it.

The doorjamb splintered, and the door swung open into a media room behind the stage.

The lights in the room chose that moment to blink out.

Dax dove through the opening and shut the door behind him, hoping to slow the progress of the smoke and flames. With only a red emergency light to guide him, he found another door at the end of the narrow room. When he tried to open the door, it only moved a few inches before something on the other side blocked it from opening further.

Smoke was quickly filling the media room.

Dax shoved his shoulder into the door and pushed as hard as he could, moving the object blocking the door enough to let him squeeze into a hallway.

He nearly tripped over a dark object on the floor only to discover the object was the body of the MC who'd been with Liliana when they'd escaped through the back door.

He felt for a pulse. When he didn't find one, his gut clenched. Whoever had created the smoke and fire had killed the MC and now had Liliana.

Dax might only have seconds to find her before she met the same fate as the MC.

CHAPTER 12

WHEN THE EXPLOSION HAPPENED, Liliana immediately dropped down, shielding the back of her neck from the expected flying debris.

None came.

Instead, smoke rose up around her, forcing her back to her feet. Her first inclination was to race off the stage into Dax's arms. He'd get her to safety.

When she turned toward the steps, flames leaped up in front of her, forcing her back.

The MC grabbed her arm. "Out the back. Hurry!" He led her to a door at the back of the stage where he fumbled with a key until he finally unlocked it and threw it open.

Smoke burned Liliana's lungs and eyes. She held her hand over her nose and mouth as she ran through the door into a room filled with electronic equipment.

The MC closed the door behind them and pushed past her to another door at the end of the narrow room. This door led out into a hallway.

He held the door for Liliana. As soon as she stepped through, the MC followed and closed the door behind them.

A figure in dark clothes and a ski mask appeared from around the corner and swung a heavy pipe at the MC's head.

The metal impacting with the man's skull made a loud cracking sound.

The MC slumped to the floor and didn't move.

Liliana cried out, "What have you done?" She tried to go to the downed man, but the big guy in black grabbed her arm and yanked her away, dragging her down the hallway, away from the MC, the ballroom, Dax and the others. He came to an intersection and turned left, pulling her along with him.

Liliana struggled to break his hold on her arm. Every time she tried to jerk her arm free, he slammed her against the wall. After the third time, he stopped and cocked the arm with the pipe.

Before he could swing, Liliana ducked, pulled out of his grasp and brought her knee up hard on his groin.

The man grunted and doubled over.

She grabbed the hand holding the pipe and twisted it behind his back, pushing it up between his shoulder blades. "Drop it!" she yelled.

When he didn't, she shoved the arm up higher.

"Drop it, or I'll break your damned arm," she warned.

He released his hold on the pipe and it fell to the ground, making a loud clattering sound.

Still holding his arm high up his back, Liliana kicked the pipe down the hallway. Then she shoved the man hard, slamming him into the wall.

When he crumpled to the floor groaning, Liliana turned and ran, hoping she was headed along a corridor, leading toward the front of the ballroom. She glanced back as she rounded a corner and ran into a man coming from the opposite direction.

She hit him so hard it knocked the wind out of her and made the man stagger backward.

He grabbed her around the waist to steady both of them.

"Thank God," she cried. "A man attacked the MC. You have to help," she said and looked up into the dull gray eyes of Tate Harris. "Oh. It's you."

"Did he hurt the guy?" Harris asked, still holding her around the waist.

"Yes. He knocked him out. We need to get him to a hospital."

"Show me," he said.

"But the attacker might come after us." She pressed her hands against Harris's chest when he didn't release his hold on her. "Let me go."

"I will." His grip around her tightened. "When I'm good and ready."

Her eyes narrowed. "Let me go, or I'll scream."

"Scream all you want. No one will hear you over the screams of the people in the ballroom."

"What do you mean?" Her heartbeat fluttered. "They're evacuating, aren't they? They have to get out. The stage is on fire and the smoke..."

"It seems your attacker has been busy locking the doors from the outside. No one can get out."

"No!" Her heart sank to the pit of her belly. Dax was in there, along with Rachel, Kujo, Six and so many others. "We have to help them." She struggled to free herself from his hold that only grew tighter. "We have to get them out."

Harris shook his head. "There's nothing we can do. He must have tampered with the sprinkler system because it didn't go off, and he used chains and locks to secure the doors. We have nothing on us to cut through them. We can't get them out in time. All we can do is leave the building before it's consumed in flame." He moved back the way she'd come, dragging Liliana along with him.

"No," she cried. "We can't leave them."

"We have to save ourselves." He wasn't leading them out. The exits were in the other direction. Already, smoke was seeping into the hallway, getting thicker with each passing minute.

Then another thought occurred to her. "But you got out." Liliana dug her heels into the floor. "How did you get out and the others are trapped?"

"It doesn't matter. If the fire doesn't kill them, they'll die of smoke inhalation. It'll be a terrible tragedy. All out of revenge."

"What are you talking about?" Liliana fought to free herself from his grasp. "Who wants revenge? You?"

He laughed. "I'll be the last person they suspect since I donated so much to your campaign. They'll look and find the real culprits. The accomplice of the man you put behind bars. The news will report they came back for revenge and then committed suicide to keep from going to jail."

"Jason Monahan's accomplice?" She felt sick at her stomach. "You were behind him planting those explosives?"

"He was just a punk, looking for his next high. He was easy to convince you were to blame for ruining his life." Harris snorted. "They'll find him swinging from the light fixture in his cell by morning." He pulled a gun from beneath his suit jacket and pressed it into her side. "Either you come with me now, or I end it here."

"If you're the only one who survives, you'll be a prime suspect." Her stomach roiled at the thought of all those people trapped inside the burning ballroom.

She had to get away and help free them before it was too late.

He shoved her forward and around the corner where the man in black was pushing to his feet. He'd removed his mask and held it in his hand, swaying. When he turned around, Liliana gasped.

Though his brown hair was shaggier than when she'd last seen him in court three years ago, she couldn't forget the thick brows and mean set to his chin.

Nolan Farley straightened to his full six feet four inches. He was the spoiled son of a wealthy ranch owner, who'd joined a white supremacist group when his daddy had cut him off. He'd gone to jail for nearly killing a man of the Shoshone tribe, just for being Shoshone.

He stared at Liliana, his lip curling in a snarl.

"Did you kill the MC?" Harris asked.

"He looked dead," Nolan answered, his tone belligerent.

"Did you check to make sure?" Harris demanded. "You can't leave witnesses."

Nolan nodded toward Liliana. "She's a witness."

Harris moved Liliana closer until they were right next to Nolan.

She could smell his sweat, and it made her want to gag.

"Do you want to kill her?" Harris asked, his tone low.

"You know I do," Nolan said.

Harris shoved Liliana toward him

Nolan caught her, spun her around and clamped his arm around her neck.

Liliana clawed at that arm that felt like steel. He'd probably spend the past three years pumping iron in the prison gym, making it all that much easier to kill her.

He tightened his hold, cutting off her air.

Liliana kicked and scratched but was no match for the big man. Her vision blurred.

"Let her go," Harris said.

Nolan's arm loosened enough Liliana caught a breath and filled her starving lungs.

"You said I could kill her," Nolan ground out.

"I changed my mind. We need to make her death look like an accident.

"No," Nolan said. "You promised I could kill her." His arm tightened on her throat.

Harris glared at the man, raised his gun and pointed it at Nolan's temple. "Let her go."

Once again, her vision blurred, Liliana was on the verge of blacking out.

"No." Nolan tightened his hold.

A loud bang pierced the fog of Liliana's mind. Nolan's arm slackened, and he fell to the ground, taking Liliana with him. He landed on top of her, trapping her beneath his big frame, crushing the air from her lungs.

Harris planted his foot on the man's shoulder and shoved hard, pushing him onto his back, freeing Liliana.

He grabbed her wrist and yanked her to her feet.

She stumbled and fell, too weak from lack of oxygen to stand or fight.

He bent, dragged her over his shoulder and carried her down the hallway that was quickly filling with thick black smoke.

Liliana faded in and out of consciousness.

It seemed that Harris stopped at doors and tested the handles.

Liliana blacked out for a moment and came to as Harris found a door that opened.

He shoved her into a storage closet. Once inside, he pulled two zip ties out of his pocket and secured her wrists behind her back. Then he bound her ankles together with the other zip tie. He shined the light from his cell phone around the storage room, found some rags and stuffed one in her mouth.

"I've wasted too much time with you already. If this building doesn't burn to the ground, at least this room will. You weren't supposed to beat Merritt in the polls. I couldn't let you win." He shoved a rag into a can of paint thinner, pulled a lighter out of his pocket and lit the end of the rag. He twisted the door lock on the inside as he left the storage room, closing the door behind him.

Liliana stared at the fire burning away at the rag.

It was the only light in the room. If it continued to burn, it would kill her. Pushing through the fog of unconsciousness, she shook her head to clear her mind and vision.

She had to stop that fire from reaching the paint thinner. With her hands tied behind her, and her ankles bound together, she managed to scoot across the floor toward the rag burning closer and closer to the open can of accelerant.

Thankfully, she'd worn high heels that had required her to strap them on. They were still on her feet and were her only hope to stop the flame from reaching the fuel inside the can.

She lifted her feet and carefully snagged the rag with one of her pointed heels. The fire licked at the soles of her shoes and her bare toes. She didn't let go but lifted the rag straight up on the point of her heel. As she did, the can wobbled and rose with the rag.

Gagging on the rag in her mouth, Liliana gently bounced her feet, hoping to work the rag free.

The rag slipped across her heel and caught. The can tipped precariously to one side, liquid sloshing inside.

The fire flared brighter the more rag it burned, getting closer to the mouth of the can.

Knowing she only had seconds to spare, she yanked the rag upward, rolled and slung it toward the door.

The movement made the can tip over. Its contents sloshed over the hem of Liliana's dress and spilled across the floor toward the burning rag.

Liliana scooted backward, away from the puddle of paint thinner, but her dress dragged in the liquid trailing it after her.

She moved as far away from the burning rag as she could get and held her breath, praying the paint thinner spill didn't reach the rag before it burned out.

The light from the burning rag reflected off the spilled liquid. The pool spread to within two inches of the rag and stopped.

Liliana let go of the breath she'd been holding. She wasn't out of the woods yet. She had to get out of the zip ties and back to the ballroom. She hoped it wasn't too late to save Dax, Rachel and the others.

Using what little light was coming from the still-burning rag, she looked around the storage room for anything she could use to break the zip ties. Her gaze fell on the metal edge of a wire storage rack.

She scooted across the floor, careful not to disturb the pool of paint thinner and backed up to the rack. For the next few minutes, she rubbed the zip tie around her wrist against the metal edge, over and over, until it snapped in two.

Once her hands were free, she yanked the rag out of her mouth, pushed to her feet and dug around in a tool kit until she found a wire cutter. She had just severed the zip tie around her ankles when the rag fire fizzled out, plunging her into complete darkness with the smell of smoke seeping through the cracks in the door.

Liliana pushed to her feet and felt her way across the small room to the door. She remembered seeing Harris twist the lock on the inside of the door. That would keep people from getting into her, but shouldn't keep her from getting out.

She gripped the handle and attempted to turn it. It didn't budge. She tried again and again. No amount of twisting would make the handle turn.

Somehow, Harris had jammed the door, trapping her inside.

Liliana kicked the door and screamed as loud as she could.

No one came. The longer she remained trapped, the less likely she'd get to the other trapped people in the ballroom in time to save them.

Nope.

She wouldn't believe it was too late to save Dax and the others. She wouldn't give up without a fight.

She ran her hands across the door to the hinges. Her heart filled with hope. The hinges were on the inside. All she had to do was remove the hinge pin and pull the door off the hinges.

Liliana felt her way back to the toolbox, found a screwdriver and a hammer. She also felt the heavy-duty metal of a pair of bolt cutters.

"I can do this," she said as she made her way back to the door.

She'd get out of that storage closet if it was the last thing she did. Then she'd find her way back to the ballroom with the bolt cutters to free the people trapped inside.

CHAPTER 13

D<small>AX LEFT</small> the MC's body and ran down the hallway until he reached an intersection of another corridor.

Which way? He looked to the right, left and straight forward. There was no sign of Liliana. She could have been taken down any of the corridors, and he didn't know which one.

He'd search all of them if he had to.

Dax turned right and sprinted down the corridor. When he came to a door, he tried the handle. Most were locked. At the end of the hallway, the last door opened into a huge laundry room.

A man wearing a white uniform was directing employees out of the area. When he saw Dax, he waved at him. "You need to get out. There's a fire in the building. Everyone needs to get out. Now."

"Have you seen a woman in a silver dress come through here?" Dax asked.

The man shook his head. "No, sir. Only employees. Sir, you need to leave the building."

Dax didn't stand around to argue. He turned and ran back the way he'd come. When he came to the intersection, he turned right. Again, none of the doors he encountered were open until he reached the end of that hallway at a set of double doors that opened into a huge room full of giant machines he suspected supported the electrical systems throughout the complex. The noise was deafening. After a quick look around the big room, he came back out and closed the doors behind him. He thought he heard a bang, but he couldn't be sure since his ears were still ringing from the noise bombardment of the machine room.

He retraced his footsteps to the intersection ready to turn left again when he noticed a man wearing a suit in the hallway, headed back toward the ballroom.

He ran after him. As he neared him, he recognized the gray pinstripe suit and salt-and-pepper gray hair of Tate Harris.

"Harris!" Dax called out as he closed in on the man.

Harris spun around as if startled by Dax's voice. Then he smiled. "Mr. Young. I didn't know you were behind me."

Dax frowned. "You got out."

Harris's brow wrinkled. "Of course, I did."

"And the others?"

"They're all safe," he said. "I was just checking to make sure no one got lost. You should head out front where the others are. It's not safe in the building. The fire hasn't been contained."

The man was too smooth, too slick with all the right answers.

Dax studied him closely. "Have you seen Liliana?"

Harris tilted his head. "I assumed she was with you." The entire time he'd been talking, he'd held his right arm close to his side as if hiding something.

The closer Dax looked the more he realized the gray pinstripe suit had little dark spots on the right arm and shoulder as if it had been sprayed by something.

His heart pinched hard in his chest.

"Where is she?" Dax asked, his tone low and dangerous. He stepped toward Harris.

"I told you, I thought she was with you." Harris moved his right arm in a flash, whipping a gun out in front of him.

Rage ripped through Dax as he stood in front of Tate Harris at gunpoint, knowing the man had blood spatter on his suit. "Where is she?" he said through gritted teeth.

"It's too late. She's gone." His eyes narrowed. "And so are you."

Dax moved so quickly that when Harris pulled the trigger, Dax had the barrel of the gun pointed at the ceiling. The bullet hit the ceiling tile, and Dax throat-punched Harris, relieving him of the weapon and leaving him gasping for air.

Dax turned the gun on Harris and shoved it under his chin. "Tell me where she is, and I might let you live."

"It's like I said...it's too late," Harris said, his voice raspy. "If the fire from the ballroom hasn't reached her, the other one will have."

"What other one?" Dax moved the barrel of the pistol to press between the man's eyes. "Bastard. If you've hurt her, I'll rip you apart, one limb at a time."

Harris sneered. "You won't shoot me."

"Where is she?" Dax hated that Harris was right. He wouldn't shoot the man, but he wasn't above hitting him.

Dax pulled the gun back and pistol-whipped the man in the face.

Harris's head jerked to the side and blood dripped from the cut on his cheek.

"Tell me," Dax demanded.

"It's too late," Harris laughed. "She shouldn't have tried playing in the big leagues."

Dax turned the gun around, ready to break every rule in his moral code book and shoot the man point blank.

"Dax!" a voice called out from the direction of the ballroom.

Dax glanced to his left.

Kujo and Six ran toward him. "Where's Liliana?"

He stopped next to Dax, his eyes narrowing when he saw who Dax had cornered.

"That's what I'm trying to find out." Dax said. "What about the people in the ballroom?"

"Everyone made it out," Kujo said. "I found the MC in the hallway." He tipped his head toward Harris. "Did he kill him?"

"That's my guess. And he knows where Liliana is but won't tell me."

"Shoot the bastard," Kujo said.

"He won't," Harris jeered. "He doesn't have it in him."

"On second thoughts, don't do it, Dax," Kujo said. "Let him go."

Dax's lips curled up, and he stood back, releasing his hold on Harris. "Okay."

Harris straightened his suit. "You made the right decision. Now, step aside."

Kujo and Dax stepped aside.

Harris's eyes narrowed as he turned and walked away, moving quickly.

Kujo let the man get a couple yards away then he said, "Six."

The German Shepherd's ears perked, and he tensed in a ready stance.

Kujo issued the command, "Attack."

Six shot forward.

Harris barely had time to look back before Six was on him, sinking his teeth into Harris's left arm.

The man screamed. "Call him off! Jesus Christ, call him off! I'll tell you where she is!"

"Six. Sit." Kujo called out.

Six growled low in his chest, released Harris's arm and returned to Kujo's side where he sat, ears up, body tense, ready for the next command.

Kujo rubbed his head. "Good boy."

Dax hurried toward Harris, grabbed his injured arm and yanked him to his feet.

The man cried out and pulled his arm free, "Watch it."

Dax gripped the man's injured arm again.

Harris swung his right fist at Dax.

Dax ducked and instinctively landed a punch in the man's face.

Harris slammed backward, hit the wall and sank to the ground.

"Damn!" Dax lifted the man up by his lapels. "Wake up, you bastard." He shook Harris. The man's head lolled. He was down for the count, and Dax still didn't know where Liliana was.

"He's the only one who knows where she is." Dax slapped the man's face. "Wake up!"

Kujo called out. "I'm pretty sure we can find her without his help."

"She could be anywhere. Most of the doors on these hallways are locked. She could be behind any one of them. Plus, he said something about another fire. We don't have time to search every damn room."

Kujo touched Six's head and spoke in a clear, distinct command, "Six, seek Liliana."

Six glanced up at Kujo then took off, nose to the ground at first. Then he ran a few steps, sniffed the ground again and ran some more.

Dax didn't like leaving Harris, but he was more concerned about finding Liliana alive. He followed Kujo and Six as they turned down the left corridor and disappeared around another corner. Dax and Kujo ran to keep up. When they rounded the second corner, they nearly tripped over the body of a man dressed all in black, with a bullet hole through his forehead. Six hadn't paused but kept going almost to the end of the corridor where the smoke was getting thicker.

Six stopped in front of a door and laid on the floor, giving a little whine, his tail wagging.

Kujo and Dax arrived at the door, skidding to a stop next to Six.

Dax tried to open the door, but the handle wouldn't turn. Something had been jammed into the door lock to keep it from working. "Liliana," Dax called out and held his breath.

"Dax!" Liliana's sweet voice sounded from the other side of the door. "Thank God."

"Are you okay?" he asked.

"Yes. But look out for Tate Harris. He's dangerous."

"We found him. He's not going to hurt anyone anytime soon."

"He killed Nolan Farley," she said. "Shot him in the face," she said.

"We found Farley," Dax said. "We're going to get you out of there."

"I think you can now," she said. "I almost had it, but couldn't get any leverage."

Dax laughed. "Sweetheart, what are you talking about?"

"I'm going to stand back. Just push really hard on the door."

"You want me to kick it in?" he said.

"I don't think you have to kick it. Try pushing first."

Dax shot a glance at Kujo.

Kujo shrugged.

"Okay, I'm pushing." He leaned on the door and pushed hard.

The door flew off its hinges and crashed to the floor inside a storage closet with Dax landing on top of it.

"Okay, so you didn't have to push that hard." Liliana helped him to his feet and threw her arms around him. "Boy, I'm glad to see you."

He leaned back and stared down into her eyes. "Not as glad as I am to see you." He kissed her hard and fast on the lips and then stared at the door. "What happened?"

"I removed the hinge pins, but I couldn't pull it off the hinges because I couldn't get my fingers between the door and the doorjamb. I felt all around in the room but couldn't find a crowbar or anything else to use as leverage." She coughed and held her hand over her mouth and nose. "We need to get out of here, and I can't be around any flames."

Dax noticed an acrid smell in the room. "What's that smell?"

"Paint thinner," Liliana said. "It's all over my dress and the floor. Harris left me zip tied in the room with a lit rag stuffed into a paint thinner can." She lifted her chin. "The man had no idea who he was dealing with. I grew up on the rez. I've been in worse situations." She reached into the room, snagged a pair of bolt cutters and turned back to Dax.

He grinned. "All of the people are safely out of the ballroom. We won't need those."

"Good." She dropped them on the floor, hooked her arm around Dax's arm and stepped over the door into the hallway.

The smoke had grown even thicker, making it hard to breathe and even harder to see.

Dax, Liliana and Kujo bent low and ran back the way they'd come. More smoke billowed from the direction of the ballroom.

Harris still lay against the wall where they'd left him.

"Should we leave him?" Kujo asked.

"The man deserves to die," Liliana said, "but that would be too kind. He needs to rot in jail for what he's done."

"And you're just the attorney that could make that happen." Dax pulled the man over his shoulder in a fireman's carry. "Follow me. I know another way out."

He led them to the laundry room and out a rear door to where the laundry room staff stood, waiting for the all-clear sign to return to work.

Dax dropped Harris on the ground, pulled out his cell phone, called Rachel and said, "We have Liliana. She's okay."

"Oh, thank God," Rachel said. "I've been beside myself with worry. Let me talk to her."

Dax handed the cell phone to Liliana. "It's for you." Then he pulled her into his arms and held her as she talked to her assistant, checking the status of the others who'd been trapped inside the ballroom.

While she talked with Rachel, Dax looked over his shoulder at Kujo. "How did you get them out?"

"The doors were blocked. The security guards had been shot. There was no way to get them out the doors."

"Then how?" Dax asked.

Kujo's lips twisted. "Let's just say we broke a lot of windows. Thankfully, the drop to the next level was only eight feet. Everyone worked together to get those less agile to the ground safely. We had a few twisted ankles, some smoke inhalation and a couple asthma attacks, but everyone made it out alive, except the two security guards."

"And the MC and Nolan Farley, one of the two men Harris hired to kill me." Liliana handed Dax's cell phone back to him. Her brow twisted. "Harris also said that Jason Monahan would be found dead in his jail cell by morning of apparent suicide. You might want to call your guys and have them check on the jail. If he lives past morning, I bet he'll talk now. Harris eliminated one of his henchmen. We need to hang onto the other for Harris's trial."

Dax stared at the unconscious man. "He needs to rot in jail for the rest of his life. Is he even alive?"

Kujo nudged the man with his foot.

Harris moaned.

"Damn. He is." Dax pulled her closer. "How is a guy supposed to save you when you can save yourself?"

She laughed, coughed and laughed again. "I don't think I would've lasted much longer in the smoke. If you hadn't found me, I'd still be in that room."

Dax smiled down at her. "I'd like to take credit for finding you, but it was Six who did all the work."

Liliana bent to scratch behind Six's ears. "Good boy."

Six nuzzled her hand and licked her fingers.

Liliana smiled and straightened, slipping back

into the circle of Dax's arm. "You know, we don't have to pretend to be engaged anymore."

His arm tightened around her. "The hell we don't. You have an election to win. I'll be with you at least through election day."

She turned into him and rested her cheek against his chest. "That's not much longer. Then what?" Liliana tipped her head up and stared into his eyes in the light from the stars shining brightly in the Wyoming night sky. "What if I don't want this to end?"

He brushed his lips across hers. All his life, he'd sworn off committing to a woman. Yet here he was after only a few days with Liliana, and he was ready to break his promise to himself with a woman whose life would make his all kinds of complicated. "It doesn't have to end." Dax couldn't believe he'd said those words. Then again, he didn't want to take them back.

"If I win the election, being with me will be..." She drew in a deep breath.

"Complicated," he said. "I know. And it won't be *if* you win. It'll be *when* you win."

"I wouldn't even begin to ask you to sacrifice your sanity for life with me. It would be too much to ask."

"Then don't ask," he said, smoothing a strand of her jet-back hair back from her cheek. "Give us the rest of this campaign to get to know each other better, then *I'll* do the asking."

She frowned up at him. "I won't hold you to it if you change your mind."

"I'm not polished or a big shot politician or businessman. I might not be what you need in your life as a congresswoman. You need to be sure I won't drag you down or hold you back. Take the time to be absolutely sure because, once I commit, I won't change my mind. I'm all in until death do us part. But I'll give you time in case you change yours."

She smiled up at him. "Not a chance."

Dax prayed she wouldn't change her mind. He was sure in his heart of his feelings. For the first time in his life, he was willing to risk his heart for a woman. But not just any woman.

He was in love with Liliana.

EPILOGUE

"D<small>ID</small> you hear Jason Monahan made a plea bargain and confessed his part in Tate Harris's scheme to kill Liliana?" Amanda stood beside Liliana, nursing a cup of coffee.

Liliana nodded. "I heard. He admitted that Harris paid him and Nolan Farley to steal the C-4 and plant it under the Riverton stage. When he found out Harris had arranged for him to *commit suicide*, he was a lot more willing to spill his guts. He didn't want to end up like Nolan."

"Stone and Swede found out that Harris was in deep with his investors, unable to deliver on his promises," Dax said. "He was losing money so fast they were ready to pull the project and his bonus, which he'd already spent on a new Ferrari and a house in California. The man was desperate."

Amanda's lips pressed into a tight line. "Desperate

enough to rig the election by eliminating the competition."

"Thankfully, I had my protector to look after me." Liliana smiled up at Dax.

He shook his head. "I almost lost you."

She leaned into him. "But you found me in time to save me from dying of smoke inhalation."

"And now we're here, and the election is over," Amanda said. "We just have to wait for the results."

Rachel set down the phone, her face devoid of any emotion. "Ladies and Gentlemen, gather around. I just got off the phone with the voting center. Ninety percent of the votes are in."

A million butterflies took flight in Liliana's belly as she joined Rachel at the center of the room.

Dax stood beside her, holding her hand, letting her squeeze it so tightly she was bound to be cutting off his circulation.

Campaign headquarters in the Wind River Indian Reservation Cultural center was a mess of empty soda cans, stacks of stained paper coffee cups, empty chip bags and half-empty boxes of donuts and cookies.

Most of Liliana's staff had been up throughout the night, monitoring election results.

Being an independent candidate put Liliana at a disadvantage, especially when so many voters liked to vote the party line, either all Republican or all Democrat.

Early on, Brad Benton fell behind and stayed behind, conceding his loss before midnight, which left Ronald Merritt and Liliana Lightfeather in the race.

Throughout the night, the results showed them running neck and neck, alternating between Merritt winning and Lightfeather winning by only a few percentage points.

Tension was so thick in the air that Liliana could have cut it with a knife.

Dax leaned close and whispered. "You're already a winner in my books."

She smiled up at him. Not only was election day the day that would decide her future career, but it would also be when she and Dax decided their future together or apart.

Since they'd promised to give each other the time to make that decision, they hadn't talked about it, focusing on her campaign instead.

Dax had been at her side at every town hall, every fundraiser and all the meet-n-greets she'd done in small and large towns. They'd ridden horses in the Cheyenne Frontier Days parade and visited veterans at Sheridan's VA Medical Center.

Not only had Liliana gotten to know more about her home state, but she had also gotten to know more about Dax, falling deeper and deeper in love with him every day.

By all indications, Dax felt the same. Only one

troubling issue remained. He hadn't said the L word once.

Then again, neither had she.

Liliana had taken her promise to heart. If he changed his mind about their relationship after election day, she wouldn't hold it against him.

She'd let him go without any drama.

Then she'd go back home, cry, scream into her pillow and bury herself in bed for a week, eating ice cream by the gallon, hoping it would freeze her heart to keep it from hurting. Losing Dax now would be...

Worse than terrible.

She didn't even want to contemplate it.

Liliana squeezed his hand, barely caring what the results were. She wanted to know if he'd changed his mind.

"As you all know, the results have fluctuated all night long," Rachel continued. "After counting the majority of the mail-in votes, one candidate has taken a decisive lead." She drew a deep breath and looked around the room, her gaze stopping when it reached Liliana. A smile spread across her face. "Miss Liliana Lightfeather, not only are you in the lead with a considerable gap, you're projected to stay in the lead until the final vote is counted."

A cheer went up around the room.

Liliana smiled and held up her hand. "I don't want to celebrate and jinx us. We need to wait until the last vote is counted or Merritt concedes."

The cheering died down to excited chatter.

The phone beside Rachel rang. She answered and listened, her brow puckering. "Yes, I understand. Thank you for letting us know." She met Liliana's questioning gaze and took her time telling her what the hell the call was about.

Liliana didn't like it when Rachel paused for effect to build anticipation. "Who was that?"

"A representative from Ronald Merritt's campaign headquarters. Merritt just conceded the election." Rachel threw her hands in the air. "You won! You won!

Once again, the room erupted in cheers. Liliana flung her arms around Rachel and hugged her tightly. "Thank you. I could not have done it without you."

Rachel wiped tears from her eyes. "I wouldn't represent just anyone. You're the real deal. You're going to make a great congresswoman."

"I'm counting on you to be by my side throughout," Liliana said.

"You can't get rid of me now." Rachel hugged her again and did a little dance.

Amanda was next, hugging her so tightly she could barely breathe. When she let go, they both did a happy dance, grinning like idiots.

Liliana turned to the people celebrating, throwing confetti and laughing out loud. "Thank you all for everything you've done to see us through this campaign. We wouldn't have won without the help of every person in this room. Thank you from the bottom of my heart.

"Now, for me, the real work begins. I promised to make a difference and be a true representative of the great state of Wyoming. I'll continue to count on you to keep me informed and grounded with the people. I love you. Thank you all."

More cheering and confetti filled the room. Liliana stayed a couple more hours to speak with news reporters about her win and her plans for the future of Wyoming.

When the last reporter left and most of her staff had gone home to bed, Liliana finally started for the exit with Dax at her side.

"Do you want to hit the diner or go straight home?" he asked.

"Home," she said. "I could sleep for a week."

"Rachel said she had a care package delivered to your house with dinner from one of the local caterers."

Liliana sighed. "I don't know what I'd do without Rachel."

"I know you're tired and want to sleep, but could you hold on a little longer? I'd like to go for a drive to unwind a little."

Suddenly awake, with sleep furthest from her mind, Liliana nodded. If this was the big decision, she'd just as soon get it over with right away. Driving around would only prolong the agony of not knowing. "I'd like that," she lied.

As they walked toward the door, she didn't reach for his hand like she had every day since the fire at the Jackson resort.

If he was going to end it, she might as well get used to no more handholding.

They were halfway across the room when he reached for her hand and held it firmly in his.

Liliana tried not to read too much into his move. It could be his way of letting her down slowly.

Oh, why did they have to go for a drive?

Schooling her face to a neutral, possibly deadpan look, she let him open the door for her and walked past him without giving him her usual smile and kiss.

Liliana's shoulder brushed against his as she climbed into his truck and buckled her seat belt.

Dax didn't say a word as he rounded the front of the truck and slid into the driver's seat. He started the truck, shifted into gear and drove out of the parking lot. He headed for the river where they'd had several picnic lunches, enjoying the beauty of the water, the sky and each other's company.

Liliana had to admit it was the right place to go for any major announcements. Good or bad.

She steeled herself for the bad, praying it would instead be good news.

Dax parked, got out of the truck and rounded to her side, where he helped her to the ground.

Still, he hadn't said a word, giving her no clue what he had in mind. By the time they reached the water's edge, Liliana's eyes stung, and her throat threatened to close as she swallowed back a rising sob.

As Dax turned her to face him, the first tear slipped down her cheek, followed by more.

His brow dipped into a frown. "What's wrong? Why the tears?" He brushed his thumb across her cheek, his frown deepening. "Is this it? Is this when you tell me you've changed your mind and don't want me to be a part of your life?" He gathered her hands in his. "Please, don't let that be the case. I've been planning this day for the past few weeks. I had it all worked out how I was going to say what I wanted to say, and now…"

"Say what?" she squeaked, that lump in her throat easing only slightly. "Tell me. What have you decided? It's killing me." More tears poured down her face.

"Oh, baby. I never meant to make you cry. I only want to love you and hold you in my arms for the rest of our lives. Please tell me you haven't changed your mind. Say something." He wiped the tears from her cheeks, his own glassy with his own unshed tears.

"No," Liliana said. "That's not it at all. I thought you brought me out here to let me down easy. I thought you wanted to end it and walk away with your sanity intact. I mean, who would willingly walk into what promises to be an insane life split between Wyoming and Washington, D.C.?"

"I would," he said softly. "So, I'm asking you for the second time, and the first real time, Liliana Lightfeather, will you marry me? Will you promise to be with me for the rest of our lives? Because you see, I love you so much that I can't imagine life without you. I'll follow you anywhere you go. If you want children, I'll give you a dozen. If you don't, I'm good with that, too. I want to love you and grow old with you."

She sniffed, her heart lighter and her smile returning. "I might be gone a lot," she warned.

He smiled. "I might be gone a lot, too. But when we're together, we'll love each other twice as hard to make up for the times apart."

Liliana laughed and smiled. "Yes, I will marry you, for real, because I love you and can't imagine my life without you in it." She laughed. "Whew! I can't believe I've won!"

"You were a shoo-in for congresswoman. I never doubted it for a minute." He kissed the tip of her nose.

"No, I won something even better. I won the lottery of love with a man who makes all my dreams come true. I love you, Daxton Young. I can't wait to begin the rest of our lives together."

"There's no better day than today to start." He

pulled her into his arms and kissed her until her toes curled and her heart soared.

Their lives might not be the easiest, but as long as they were together, they'd figure it out.

Love would win every time.

SAVING BREELY

BROTHERHOOD PROTECTORS
YELLOWSTONE BOOK #5

New York Times & *USA Today*
Bestselling Author

ELLE JAMES

YELLOWSTONE
SAVING BREELY

BROTHERHOOD PROTECTORS

New York Times & USA Today Bestselling Author
ELLE JAMES

ABOUT SAVING BREELY

THE PROTECTOR

FORMER AIR FORCE PARAJUMPER, MORRIS "MOE" Cleveland might be smaller than the other members of his team, but size, in his case, certainly matters. He can fit in places his counterparts can't and his body is wiry, streamlined and fast. The perfect choice when it comes to proportional matches. Thankfully, his new client is nine inches shorter than him.

Assigned to protection duty for a rich man's daughter seems a waste of his skills. But he's getting paid well for babysitting duty and wouldn't complain. At least he isn't dodging bullets in the Middle East. Instead, he's dodging his growing feelings for the feisty redhead.

. . .

The Client

When her little brother died of leukemia, Breely's parents hovered over her, refusing to let her do things for fear of losing their only living child. Breely rebelled against the suffocation, moved off the family ranch and into her own place in Eagle Rock. She lives a double life. By day she's the face of Brantt enterprises, managing her father's philanthropic ventures. At night she moonlights as Bea, the feisty waitress at the Blue Moose Tavern. Breely made a vow to herself to live a real life, not one cocooned in bubble wrap, protected from every which way the wind might blows.

WHEN SHE'S TARGETED by kidnappers, she is forced to accept help from a regular at the bar who, with his Brotherhood Protectors team's blessing is assigned as her bodyguard. As Breely's world goes sideways, she learns she might live longer if someone with mad combat skills has her back. Surrounded by danger, she finds safety, warmth and heart in her protector's arms.

Pre-Order Saving Breely here!

BREAKING SILENCE

DELTA FORCE STRONG BOOK #1

New York Times & *USA Today*
Bestselling Author

ELLE JAMES

BREAKING Silence

DELTA FORCE · STRONG

New York Times & USA Today Bestselling Author

ELLE JAMES

CHAPTER 1

HAD he known they would be deployed so soon after their last short mission to El Salvador, Rucker Sloan wouldn't have bought that dirt bike from his friend Duff. Now, it would sit there for months before he actually got to take it out to the track.

The team had been given forty-eight hours to pack their shit, take care of business and get onto the C130 that would transport them to Afghanistan.

Now, boots on the ground, duffel bags stowed in their assigned quarters behind the wire, they were ready to take on any mission the powers that be saw fit to assign.

What he wanted most that morning, after being awake for the past thirty-six hours, was a cup of strong, black coffee.

The rest of his team had hit the sack as soon as they got in. Rucker had already met with their commanding officer, gotten a brief introduction to the regional issues and had been told to get some rest. They'd be operational within the next forty-eight hours.

Too wound up to sleep, Rucker followed a stream of people he hoped were heading for the chow hall. He should be able to get coffee there.

On the way, he passed a sand volleyball court where two teams played against each other. One of the teams had four players, the other only three. The four-person squad slammed a ball to the ground on the other side of the net. The only female player ran after it as it rolled toward Rucker.

He stopped the ball with his foot and picked it up.

The woman was tall, slender, blond-haired and blue-eyed. She wore an Army PT uniform of shorts and an Army T-shirt with her hair secured back from her face in a ponytail seated on the crown of her head.

Without makeup, and sporting a sheen of perspiration, she was sexy as hell, and the men on both teams knew it.

They groaned when Rucker handed her the ball. He'd robbed them of watching the female soldier bending over to retrieve the runaway.

She took the ball and frowned. "Do you play?"

"I have," he answered.

"We could use a fourth." She lifted her chin in challenge.

Tired from being awake for the past thirty-six hours, Rucker opened his mouth to say *hell no*. But he made the mistake of looking into her sky-blue eyes and instead said, "I'm in."

What the hell was he thinking?

Well, hadn't he been wound up from too many hours sitting in transit? What he needed was a little physical activity to relax his mind and muscles. At least, that's what he told himself in the split-second it took to step into the sandbox and serve up a heaping helping of whoop-ass.

He served six times before the team playing opposite finally returned one. In between each serve, his side gave him high-fives, all members except one—the blonde with the blue eyes he stood behind, admiring the length of her legs beneath her black Army PT shorts.

Twenty minutes later, Rucker's team won the match. The teams broke up and scattered to get showers or breakfast in the chow hall.

"Can I buy you a cup of coffee?" the pretty blonde asked.

"Only if you tell me your name." He twisted his lips into a wry grin. "I'd like to know who delivered those wicked spikes."

She held out her hand. "Nora Michaels," she said.

He gripped her hand in his, pleased to feel firm pressure. Women might be the weaker sex, but he didn't like a dead fish handshake from males or females. Firm and confident was what he preferred. Like her ass in those shorts.

She cocked an eyebrow. "And you are?"

He'd been so intent thinking about her legs and ass, he'd forgotten to introduce himself. "Rucker Sloan. Just got in less than an hour ago."

"Then you could probably use a tour guide to the nearest coffee."

He nodded. "Running on fumes here. Good coffee will help."

"I don't know about good, but it's coffee and it's fresh." She released his hand and fell in step beside him, heading in the direction of some of the others from their volleyball game.

"As long as it's strong and black, I'll be happy."

She laughed. "And awake for the next twenty-four hours."

"Spoken from experience?" he asked, casting a glance in her direction.

She nodded. "I work nights in the medical facility. It can be really boring and hard to stay awake when we don't have any patients to look after." She held up her hands. "Not that I want any of our boys injured and in need of our care."

"But it does get boring," he guessed.

"It makes for a long deployment." She held out her hand. "Nice to meet you, Rucker. Is Rucker a call sign or your real name?"

He grinned. "Real name. That was the only thing

my father gave me before he cut out and left my mother and me to make it on our own."

"Your mother raised you, and you still joined the Army?" She raised an eyebrow. "Most mothers don't want their boys to go off to war."

"It was that or join a gang and end up dead in a gutter," he said. "She couldn't afford to send me to college. I was headed down the gang path when she gave me the ultimatum. Join and get the GI-Bill, or she would cut me off and I'd be out in the streets. To her, it was the only way to get me out of L.A. and to have the potential to go to college someday."

She smiled "And you stayed in the military."

He nodded. "I found a brotherhood that was better than any gang membership in LA. For now, I take college classes online. It was my mother's dream for me to graduate college. She never went, and she wanted so much more for me than the streets of L.A.. When my gig is up with the Army, if I haven't finished my degree, I'll go to college fulltime."

"And major in what?" Nora asked.

"Business management. I'm going to own my own security service. I want to put my combat skills to use helping people who need dedicated and specialized protection."

Nora nodded. "Sounds like a good plan."

"I know the protection side of things. I need to learn the business side and business law. Life will be different on the civilian side."

"True."

"How about you? What made you sign up?" he asked.

She shrugged. "I wanted to put my nursing degree to good use and help our men and women in uniform. This is my first assignment after training."

"Drinking from the firehose?" Rucker stopped in front of the door to the mess hall.

She nodded. "Yes. But it's the best baptism under fire medical personnel can get. I'll be a better nurse for it when I return to the States."

"How much longer do you have to go?" he asked, hoping that she'd say she'd be there as long as he was. In his case, he never knew how long their deployments would last. One week, one month, six months…

She gave him a lopsided smile. "I ship out in a week."

"That's too bad." He opened the door for her. "I just got here. That doesn't give us much time to get to know each other."

"That's just as well." Nora stepped through the door. "I don't want to be accused of fraternizing. I'm too close to going back to spoil my record."

Rucker chuckled. "Playing volleyball and sharing a table while drinking coffee won't get you written up. I like the way you play. I'm curious to know where you learned to spike like that."

"I guess that's reasonable. Coffee first." She led him into the chow hall.

The smells of food and coffee made Rucker's mouth water.

He grabbed a tray and loaded his plate with eggs, toast and pancakes drenched in syrup. Last, he stopped at the coffee urn and filled his cup with freshly brewed black coffee.

When he looked around, he found Nora seated at one of the tables, holding a mug in her hands, a small plate with cottage cheese and peaches on it.

He strode over to her. "Mind if I join you?"

"As long as you don't hit on me," she said with cocked eyebrows.

"You say that as if you've been hit on before."

She nodded and sipped her steaming brew. "I lost count how many times in the first week I was here."

"Shows they have good taste in women and, unfortunately, limited manners."

"And you're better?" she asked, a smile twitching the corners of her lips.

"I'm not hitting on you. You can tell me to leave, and I'll be out of this chair so fast, you won't have time to enunciate the V."

She stared straight into his eyes, canted her head to one side and said, "Leave."

In the middle of cutting into one of his pancakes, Rucker dropped his knife and fork on the tray, shot out of his chair and left with his tray, sloshing coffee as he moved. He hoped she was just testing him. If she wasn't...oh, well. He was used to eating meals alone. If she was, she'd have to come to him.

He took a seat at the next table, his back to her, and resumed cutting into his pancake.

Nora didn't utter a word behind him.

Oh, well. He popped a bite of syrupy sweet pancake in his mouth and chewed thoughtfully. She was only there for another week. Man, she had a nice ass...and those legs... He sighed and bent over his plate to stab his fork into a sausage link.

"This chair taken?" a soft, female voice sounded in front of him.

He looked up to see the pretty blond nurse standing there with her tray in her hands, a crooked smile on her face.

He lifted his chin in silent acknowledgement.

She laid her tray on the table and settled onto the chair. "I didn't think you'd do it."

"Fair enough. You don't know me," he said.

"I know that you joined the Army to get out of street life. That your mother raised you after your father skipped out, that you're working toward a business degree and that your name is Rucker." She sipped her coffee.

He nodded, secretly pleased she'd remembered all that. Maybe there was hope for getting to know the pretty nurse before she redeployed to the States. And who knew? They might run into each other on the other side of the pond.

Still, he couldn't show too much interest, or he'd be no better than the other guys who'd hit on her. "Since you're redeploying back to the States in a week, and I'm due to go out on a mission, probably within the next twenty-four to forty-eight hours, I don't know if it's worth our time to get to know each other any more than we already have."

She nodded. "I guess that's why I want to sit with you. You're not a danger to my perfect record of no fraternizing. I don't have to worry that you'll fall in love with me in such a short amount of time." She winked.

He chuckled. "As I'm sure half of this base has fallen in love with you since you've been here."

She shrugged. "I don't know if it's love, but it's damned annoying."

"How so?"

She rolled her eyes toward the ceiling. "I get flowers left on my door every day."

"And that's annoying? I'm sure it's not easy coming up with flowers out here in the desert." He set down his fork and took up his coffee mug. "I think it's sweet." He held back a smile. Well, almost.

"They're hand-drawn on notepad paper and left on the door of my quarters and on the door to the shower tent." She shook her head. "It's kind of creepy and stalkerish."

Rucker nodded. "I see your point. The guys should at least have tried their hands at origami flowers, since the real things are scarce around here."

Nora smiled. "I'm not worried about the pictures, but the line for sick call is ridiculous."

"How so?"

"So many of the guys come up with the lamest excuses to come in and hit on me. I asked to work the nightshift to avoid sick call altogether."

"You have a fan group." He smiled. "Has the adoration gone to your head?"

She snorted softly. "No."

"You didn't get this kind of reaction back in the States?"

"I haven't been on active duty for long. I only decided to join the Army after my mother passed away. I was her fulltime nurse for a couple years as she went through stage four breast cancer. We thought she might make it." Her shoulders sagged. "But she didn't."

"I'm sorry to hear that. My mother meant a lot to me, as well. I sent money home every month after I enlisted and kept sending it up until the day she died suddenly of an aneurysm."

"I'm so sorry about your mother's passing," Nora said, shaking her head. "Wow. As an enlisted man, how did you make enough to send some home?"

"I ate in the chow hall and lived on post. I didn't

party or spend money on civilian clothes or booze. Mom needed it. I gave it to her."

"You were a good son to her," Nora said.

His chest tightened. "She died of an aneurysm a couple of weeks before she was due to move to Texas where I'd purchased a house for her."

"Wow. And, let me guess, you blame yourself for not getting her to Texas sooner...?" Her gaze captured his.

Her words hit home, and he winced. "Yeah. I should've done it sooner."

"Can't bring people back with regrets." Nora stared into her coffee cup. "I learned that. The only thing I could do was move forward and get on with living. I wanted to get away from Milwaukee and the home I'd shared with my mother. Not knowing where else to go, I wandered past a realtor's office and stepped into a recruiter's office. I had my nursing degree, they wanted and needed nurses on active duty. I signed up, they put me through some officer training and here I am." She held her arms out.

"Playing volleyball in Afghanistan, working on your tan during the day and helping soldiers at night." Rucker gave her a brief smile. "I, for one, appreciate what you're doing for our guys and gals."

"I do the best I can," she said softly. "I just wish I could do more. I'd rather stay here than redeploy back to the States, but they're afraid if they keep us here too long, we'll burn out or get PTSD."

"One week, huh?"

She nodded. "One week."

"In my field, one week to redeploy back to the States is a dangerous time. Anything can happen and usually does."

"Yeah, but you guys are on the frontlines, if not behind enemy lines. I'm back here. What could happen?"

Rucker flinched. "Oh, sweetheart, you didn't just say that..." He glanced around, hoping no one heard her tempt fate with those dreaded words *What could happen?*

Nora grinned. "You're not superstitious, are you?"

"In what we do, we can't afford not to be," he said, tossing salt over his shoulder.

"I'll be fine," she said in a reassuring, nurse's voice.

"Stop," he said, holding up his hand. "You're only digging the hole deeper." He tossed more salt over his other shoulder.

Nora laughed.

"Don't laugh." He handed her the saltshaker. "Do it."

"I'm not tossing salt over my shoulder. Someone has to clean the mess hall."

Rucker leaned close and shook salt over her shoulder. "I don't know if it counts if someone else throws salt over your shoulder, but I figure you now need every bit of luck you can get."

"You're a fighter but afraid of a little bad luck."

Nora shook her head. "Those two things don't seem to go together."

"You'd be surprised how easily my guys are freaked by the littlest things."

"And you," she reminded him.

"You asking *what could happen?* isn't a little thing. That's in-your-face tempting fate." Rucker was laying it on thick to keep her grinning, but deep down, he believed what he was saying. And it didn't make a difference the amount of education he had or the statistics that predicted outcomes. His gut told him she'd just tempted fate with her statement. Maybe he was overthinking things. Now, he was worried she wouldn't make it back to the States alive.

NORA LIKED RUCKER. He was the first guy who'd walked away without an argument since she'd arrived at the base in Afghanistan. He'd meant what he'd said and proved it. His dark brown hair and deep green eyes, coupled with broad shoulders and a narrow waist, made him even more attractive. Not all the men were in as good a shape as Rucker. And he seemed to have a very determined attitude.

She hadn't known what to expect when she'd deployed. Being the center of attention of almost every single male on the base hadn't been one of her expectations. She'd only ever considered herself average in the looks department. But when the men outnumbered women by more than ten to one, she guessed average appearance moved up in the ranks.

"Where did you learn to play volleyball?" Rucker asked, changing the subject of her leaving and her flippant comment about what could happen in one week.

"I was on the volleyball team in high school. It got me a scholarship to a small university in my home state of Minnesota, where I got my Bachelor of Science degree in Nursing."

"It takes someone special to be a nurse," he stated. "Is that what you always wanted to be?"

She shook her head. "I wanted to be a firefighter when I was in high school."

"What made you change your mind?"

She stared down at the coffee growing cold in her mug. "My mother was diagnosed with cancer when I was a senior in high school. I wanted to help but felt like I didn't know enough to be of assistance." She looked up. "She made it through chemo and radiation treatments and still came to all of my volleyball games. I thought she was in the clear."

"She wasn't?" Rucker asked, his tone low and gentle.

"She didn't tell me any different. When I got the scholarship, I told her I wanted to stay close to home to be with her. She insisted I go and play volleyball for the university. I was pretty good and played for the first two years I was there. I quit the team in my third year to start the nursing program. I didn't know there was anything wrong back home. I called every week to talk to Mom. She never let on that she was sick." She forced a smile. "But you don't want my sob story. You probably want to know what's going on around here."

He set his mug on the table. "If we were alone in a coffee bar back in the States, I'd reach across the table and take your hand."

"Oh, please. Don't do that." She looked around the mess hall, half expecting someone might have overheard Rucker's comment. "You're enlisted. I'm an officer. That would get us into a whole lot of trouble."

"Yeah, but we're also two human beings. I wouldn't be human if I didn't feel empathy for you and want to provide comfort."

She set her coffee cup on the table and laid her hands in her lap. "I'll be satisfied with the thought. Thank you."

"Doesn't seem like enough. When did you find out your mother was sick?"

She swallowed the sadness that welled in her throat every time she remembered coming home to find out her mother had been keeping her illness from her. "It wasn't until I went home for Christmas in my senior year that I realized she'd been lying to me for a while." She laughed in lieu of sobbing. "I don't care who they are, old people don't always tell the truth."

"How long had she been keeping her sickness from you?"

"She'd known the cancer had returned halfway through my junior year. I hadn't gone home that summer because I'd been working hard to get my coursework and clinical hours in the nursing program. When I went home at Christmas..." Nora gulped. "She wasn't the same person. She'd lost so much weight and looked twenty years older."

"Did you stay home that last semester?" Rucker asked.

"Mom insisted I go back to school and finish what I'd started. Like your mother, she hadn't gone to college. She wanted her only child to graduate. She was afraid that if I stayed home to take care of her, I wouldn't finish my nursing degree."

"I heard from a buddy of mine that those programs can be hard to get into," he said. "I can see why she wouldn't want you to drop everything in your life to take care of her."

Nora gave him a watery smile. "That's what she said. As soon as my last final was over, I returned to my hometown. I became her nurse. She lasted another three months before she slipped away."

"That's when you joined the Army?"

She shook her head. "Dad was so heartbroken, I stayed a few months until he was feeling better. I got a job at a local emergency room. On weekends, my father and I worked on cleaning out the house and getting it ready to put on the market."

"Is your dad still alive?" Rucker asked.

Nora nodded. "He lives in Texas. He moved to a small house with a big backyard." She forced a smile. "He has a garden, and all the ladies in his retirement community think he's the cat's meow. He still misses Mom, but he's getting on with his life."

Rucker tilted his head. "When did you join the military?"

"When Dad sold the house and moved into his retirement community. I worried about him, but he's doing better."

"And you?"

"I miss her. But she'd whip my ass if I wallowed in self-pity for more than a moment. She was a strong woman and expected me to be the same."

Rucker grinned. "From what I've seen, you are."

Nora gave him a skeptical look. "You've only seen me playing volleyball. It's just a game." Not that she'd admit it, but she was a real softy when it came to caring for the sick and injured.

"If you're half as good at nursing, which I'm willing to bet you are, you're amazing." He started to reach across the table for her hand. Before he actually touched her, he grabbed the saltshaker and shook it over his cold breakfast.

"You just got in this morning?" Nora asked.

Rucker nodded.

"How long will you be here?" she asked.

"I don't know."

"What do you mean, you don't know? I thought when people were deployed, they were given a specific timeframe."

"Most people are. We're deployed where and when needed."

Nora frowned. "What are you? Some kind of special forces team?"

His lips pressed together. "Can't say."

She sat back. He was some kind of Special Forces. "Army, right?"

He nodded.

That would make him Delta Force. The elite of the elite. A very skilled soldier who undertook incredibly dangerous missions. She gulped and stopped herself from reaching across the table to take his hand. "Well, I hope all goes well while you and your team are here."

"Thanks."

A man hurried across the chow hall wearing shorts and an Army T-shirt. He headed directly toward their table.

Nora didn't recognize him. "Expecting some-one?" she asked Rucker, tipping her head toward the man.

Rucker turned, a frown pulling his eyebrows together. "Why the hell's Dash awake?"

Nora frowned. "Dash? Please tell me that's his callsign, not his real name."

Rucker laughed. "It should be his real name. He's first into the fight, and he's fast." Rucker stood and faced his teammate. "What's up?"

"CO wants us all in the Tactical Operations Center," Dash said. "On the double."

"Guess that's my cue to exit." Rucker turned to Nora. "I enjoyed our talk."

She nodded. "Me, too."

Dash grinned. "Tell you what...I'll stay and finish your conversation while you see what the commander wants."

Rucker hooked Dash's arm twisted it up behind his back, and gave him a shove toward the door. "You heard the CO, he wants all of us." Rucker winked at Nora. "I hope to see you on the volleyball court before you leave."

"Same. Good luck." Nora's gaze followed Rucker's broad shoulders and tight ass out of the chow hall. Too bad she'd only be there another week before she shipped out. She would've enjoyed more volleyball and coffee with the Delta Force operative.

He'd probably be on maneuvers that entire week.

She stacked her tray and coffee cup in the collection area and left the chow hall, heading for the building where she shared her quarters with Beth Drennan, a nurse she'd become friends with during their deployment together.

As close as they were, Nora didn't bring up her conversation with the Delta. With only a week left at the base, she probably wouldn't run into him again. Though she would like to see him again, she prayed he didn't end up in the hospital.

Breaking Silence (#1)

ABOUT THE AUTHOR

ELLE JAMES also writing as MYLA JACKSON is a *New York Times* and *USA Today* Bestselling author of books including cowboys, intrigues and paranormal adventures that keep her readers on the edges of their seats. When she's not at her computer, she's traveling, snow skiing, boating, or riding her ATV, dreaming up new stories. Learn more about Elle James at www.ellejames.com

Website | Facebook | Twitter | GoodReads | Newsletter | BookBub | Amazon

Or visit her alter ego Myla Jackson at mylajackson.com
Website | Facebook | Twitter | Newsletter

Follow Me!
www.ellejames.com
ellejamesauthor@gmail.com

ALSO BY ELLE JAMES

Shadow Assassin

Delta Force Strong

Brotherhood Protectors Yellowstone

Brotherhood Protectors Colorado

SEAL Salvation (#1)

Rocky Mountain Rescue (#2)

Ranger Redemption (#3)

Tactical Takeover (#4)

Colorado Conspiracy (#5)

Rocky Mountain Madness (#6)

Free Fall (#7)

Colorado Cold Case (#8)

Fool's Folly (#9)

Brotherhood Protectors

Montana SEAL (#1)

Bride Protector SEAL (#2)

Montana D-Force (#3)

Cowboy D-Force (#4)

Montana Ranger (#5)

Montana Dog Soldier (#6)

Montana SEAL Daddy (#7)

Montana Ranger's Wedding Vow (#8)

Montana SEAL Undercover Daddy (#9)

Cape Cod SEAL Rescue (#10)

Montana SEAL Friendly Fire (#11)

Montana SEAL's Mail-Order Bride (#12)

SEAL Justice (#13)

Iron Horse Legacy

Tactical Force (#5)

Disruptive Force (#6)

Mission: Six

One Intrepid SEAL

Two Dauntless Hearts

Three Courageous Words

Four Relentless Days

Five Ways to Surrender

Six Minutes to Midnight

Hearts & Heroes Series

Wyatt's War (#1)

Mack's Witness (#2)

Ronin's Return (#3)

Sam's Surrender (#4)

Take No Prisoners Series

SEAL's Honor (#1)

SEAL'S Desire (#2)

SEAL's Embrace (#3)

SEAL's Obsession (#4)

SEAL's Proposal (#5)

SEAL's Seduction (#6)

SEAL'S Defiance (#7)

Hot Velocity (#4)

Cajun Magic Mystery Series

Voodoo on the Bayou (#1)

Voodoo for Two (#2)

Deja Voodoo (#3)

Cajun Magic Mysteries Books 1-3

SEAL Of My Own

Navy SEAL Survival

Navy SEAL Captive

Navy SEAL To Die For

Navy SEAL Six Pack

Devil's Shroud Series

Deadly Reckoning (#1)

Deadly Engagement (#2)

Deadly Liaisons (#3)

Deadly Allure (#4)

Deadly Obsession (#5)

Deadly Fall (#6)

Covert Cowboys Inc Series

Triggered (#1)

Taking Aim (#2)

Bodyguard Under Fire (#3)

Cowboy Resurrected (#4)

Navy SEAL Justice (#5)

Navy SEAL Newlywed (#6)

High Country Hideout (#7)

Clandestine Christmas (#8)

Thunder Horse Series

Hostage to Thunder Horse (#1)

Thunder Horse Heritage (#2)

Thunder Horse Redemption (#3)

Christmas at Thunder Horse Ranch (#4)

Demon Series

Hot Demon Nights (#1)

Demon's Embrace (#2)

Tempting the Demon (#3)

Lords of the Underworld

Witch's Initiation (#1)

Witch's Seduction (#2)

The Witch's Desire (#3)

Possessing the Witch (#4)

Stealth Operations Specialists (SOS)

Nick of Time

Alaskan Fantasy

Boys Behaving Badly Anthologies

Rogues (#1)

Blue Collar (#2)

Pirates (#3)

Stranded (#4)

First Responder (#5)

Blown Away

Warrior's Conquest

Enslaved by the Viking Short Story

Conquests

Smokin' Hot Firemen

Protecting the Colton Bride

Protecting the Colton Bride & Colton's Cowboy Code

Heir to Murder

Secret Service Rescue

High Octane Heroes

Haunted

Engaged with the Boss

Cowboy Brigade

Time Raiders: The Whisper

Bundle of Trouble

Killer Body

Operation XOXO

An Unexpected Clue

Baby Bling

Under Suspicion, With Child

Texas-Size Secrets

Cowboy Sanctuary

Lakota Baby

Dakota Meltdown

Beneath the Texas Moon

Made in the USA
Middletown, DE
02 January 2023

20959426R00139